Marji's Books

The Christmas Tree Treasure Hunt

Grime Fighter Series

Grime Beat

Grime Wave

Grime Spree

Grime Family

Grime & Punishment

Heath's Point Suspense

Counter Point

Breaking Point

Boiling Point (coming soon)

Flash Point (coming soon)

Dallas Duets Clean Billionaire Romance

Ain't Misbehaving

Cry Me a River (coming soon)

Puttin' on the Ritz (coming soon)

Grime Family

**Grime Fighter Mystery
Book #4**

Marji Laine

Grime Family
Second Edition
© 2019 Marji Laine
ISBN: 978-1-944120-94-8

Faith Driven Book Production Services
Find out more about the author: *Marji Laine.com*
Or email her at: *AuthorMarjiLaine@gmail.com*

Printed in the United States of America.

I'm truly blessed with an amazing family!
They work together to give me writing time
and constantly support my career.
I dedicate this book to my youngest child
by only eleven minutes.

Brittany
Beautiful, Unique
Inspiring, Joke-Cracking, Day-Brightening
Focused on Following Christ
Spunky

This lady refuses to let me get down,
and she's my number one
Facebook fan!

"But all things become visible when they are exposed by the light, for everything that becomes visible is light.

Therefore, be careful how you walk,
not as unwise men but as wise, making the most of your time, because the days are evil."

Ephesians 5:13, 15-16

Chapter One

Matthew Donaldson's name on her phone ID meant trouble. No, more like impending doom.

Dani Foster put the phone to her ear, trying to assume a light tone. After all, her boyfriend, Jay, shared the front seat of his new Tahoe with her. "I didn't expect to hear from you, especially not this weekend." She pressed her volume button down, hoping Jay hadn't heard even a hint of the other man's voice.

"You have to come in." Matt's typical monotone was brusque, all-business.

"Yes, I'm enjoying the break. Nice to get away

from work for a few days." Matt had given permission. Surely he remembered where she had gone.

"Never mind that. There's been a slight change." His tenor voice wiggled a bit.

This wasn't good, but with Jay maneuvering the driveway of his parents' property in East Texas, there wasn't a lot she could do about changes. And hardly anything she could utter out loud. "That's right, I'll be here until Tuesday, so I really can't visit with you until then."

Jay pulled to a stop and glanced at her. "Everything all right?"

She nodded. "Insurance salesman." She muffled her whisper with her hand over the phone's speaker. Lying had become way too easy, but it still pinged her with regret.

Matthew blew his exhale through the speaker. "Fine. Have it your own way. But you need to know that our mutual friend is no longer at his current residence."

Ice slipped all the way up her spine and spread across her shoulders. *God, please don't let this start again.* "Well, okay. Um… I guess I'll have to get back to you on that. Maybe as I'm coming back into town."

"Make sure you let me know before you get here. Better yet, you stay in… Mayberry… until you hear from me."

She couldn't stay here. Couldn't put Jay's family in danger. And what if they learned about…? "That's going to be tight."

"Not playing with you. Do as I say." Matthew hung up the phone.

She let the phone droop from her ear and stared at a nameplate on the black dashboard of Jay's new car. "Sure will… I'll call you as soon as I'm back in town…. Yes, sir. And thank you." She slipped her phone into her over-sized bag and glanced at Jay. "Sorry about that." Sorry on so many levels.

"It's all right." He pointed to the end of the drive. A sprawling brick home complete with wraparound porch, gables, and a cobblestone walkway. "The folks sold my grandfather's farm and bought the place a few years ago."

"This is beautiful." She caught her breath at the iconic flower beds as she climbed out on her side. Pine trees grew along the fence line about fifty yards away. A manicured lawn sloped downward to a boathouse. "Private lake, even?"

He nodded. "Dad calls it a ranch because he has a few cows, but I think of it as more of a retreat."

"Do the cows make it a ranch?" She joined him at the back of the SUV and pulled her lightweight suitcase from the hold.

He chuckled. "Grandpa had at least a dozen, but it was still a farm. I think Dad just likes the sound of it."

A man with Jay's Native American coloring approached the porch rail and waved.

Jay returned the gesture. "That's my dad." He put his hand to her back.

"You don't look much like him. Well, except the obvious."

"I look exactly like my grandpa, my mom's father, except for my Comanche coloring." He escorted her up the steps where a woman about her height with curly, salt-and-pepper hair came out the front door. She had Jay's eyes—a much lighter version—but they were easy to recognize. "There's my boy." She reached to kiss his cheek.

Dani's heart warmed. This was what having a mom was about.

"Caroline Hunter." She turned to Dani and took both of her hands and gave them a squeeze. "And you must be Danielle."

"Dan…" Dani halted the correction. "It's so nice to meet you, Mrs. Hunter."

"And this is my dad, John Hunter." Jay gave the man a half hug.

"I'm glad you were able to visit us." He offered a tight smile and shook her hand before ushering her toward the front door.

"Thank you so much for extending the invitation for your Fourth of July party. I've never actually been to a place like this." She and her dad had lived in a condo, before his death, on the edge of a large downtown area. And now she shared an apartment in the suburbs. Rural homes like this made her think of pioneer stories.

Mrs. Hunter led her into the entry hall. "A ranch, or East Texas in general?"

"Both." She admired the chandelier hanging from the vaulted ceiling. Jay had never mentioned his parents being wealthy, but homes like this, at least where she'd been raised, were only available to celebs and the ultra-rich. "I had a pony ride at a friend's birthday party one time, but I've never been anywhere that would remotely be called country."

"Hopefully this won't seem strange for long, though you'll find it uncomfortably quiet if you're a true city girl." She took Dani's elbow. "How 'bout the nickel tour?"

She walked Dani through the lower floor, identifying Jay in family photos in the great room and showing her grandmother's china in the dining room. She merely pointed in the direction of the master suite, then led her through a formal living room to the large kitchen. "I could practically live in this room." Mrs. Hunter clearly loved cooking. She breezed around the large room as she shared details of her stove and the built-in appliances.

Dani attempted the correct responses, but cooking meant little to her. She did like the view, though. Broad windows showed an outdoor kitchen of stainless steel and stone in a covered patio.

The beauty of the house didn't seem to have an end. Three suites upstairs along with a media room gave way to a finished attic with a large office. Dani followed her to the lower floor. "What an amazing home. Did you have it custom built?" And how did a country sheriff make enough for a mansion of this caliber?

"Oh, my, no." Mrs. Hunter led her back into

the kitchen where she set up a tray with lemonade and ice-filled glasses. "The couple who built it had made a fortune in real estate. They wanted to raise race horses, but the man was murdered not long after they moved here."

"That's so sad."

"What's worse is that all of the evidence pointed toward his wife."

That would be the most obvious option. "Had she killed him?"

"No. Even though the evidence leaned that way, John gave her the benefit of the doubt and kept looking for other options." She added a plateful of cookies and picked up the tray. "Let's go out onto the front porch. Good breeze out there this time of day."

Downright windy in Dani's opinion, but she followed. Her thoughts went back to Mrs. Hunter's story. "So your husband found the real killer."

Mrs. Hunter nodded. "Was the man who had been his business partner, trying to obtain a loan from him. He lost his temper when the answer was no."

"Wow." How had he figured all of that out?

"The wife was so grateful, she offered her home to us for less than half of what it's worth. Probably closer to a third of its value. She only wanted to return to her friends and family in California."

"I bet. Get as far away from the tragedy as possible." Certainly what Dani would do. What she had done, in fact. She took a seat on a cushioned divan as her man strolled with his dad across the yard.

Her phone conversation with Matthew came back into mind. If what he'd said was true, her whole life might be in for another permanent change. One that wouldn't include Jay Hunter.

Jay glanced to where his mom and Dani had settled on the porch. Perfect. Mom was her charming self as always. *God, please work through this visit.*

Dani still had trust issues. Still had secrets, too, as far as he could tell. He'd tried backing off and letting her get to know him, but she resisted fully confiding in him. Hopefully a dose of hometown comfort and the embrace from his parents would convince her to release her doubts.

No matter what pain she'd had in the past, he would never hurt her and would do his best to protect her. Though he hadn't always succeeded in that.

He scanned her beautiful face. It had only been a week, but the swelling and bruises were all-but erased from her cheeks. Her rich, brown hair curled slightly over her forehead and hung long in waves on the sides of her face. While he liked the cute ponytail she usually wore, especially on the job, he preferred this enticing look. He jogged up the steps to join them.

"Your mom told me how they came to own

their ranch." She smiled, yet he could sense her nerves.

"That was an amazing blessing." Jay stroked his fingers through her hair hanging down her back.

"An intriguing mystery as well." Dad leaned against the rail behind his wife.

"Dad has a ton of stories. I still don't know why you stepped down from the sheriff's office."

"I would love to hear more of your stories, Mr. Hunter."

"Dani has a deep curious streak." He rubbed her back again and chuckled. "If you have any unsolved mysteries, she'll probably be able to help you out."

Dad shifted in his seat. Something like an invisible wall went up along with his stiffened shoulders. That was odd.

"I don't have anything needing her skills. I'm only a rancher, now." He pulled his phone from his pocket and wandered toward the edge of the porch with the cell to his ear.

Jay cleared his throat, feeling heat on his neck. What was with Dad? Even Mom had reddened. After an awkward pause, he turned toward her. She'd engage easier anyway. "Tell me the news, Mom." He moved to sit on the wicker couch between her and Dani and picked up a glass of lemonade. "You know you want to share all the gossip."

She gave a nervous laugh. "Oh, you know Marseilles. Always some scandal going on." Her eyes flitted to the left as she lifted her lemonade. "And I don't want Dani to believe I'm a gossip. You should take her to the town and introduce her to your friends. She'll hear plenty there."

In time, but he'd rather Dani get comfortable right here. "Maybe tonight."

"That reminds me. I'm short a few bags of chips." She set down her glass and looked up at him. "Will y'all run an errand for me?"

He glanced from her to Dani and back. "I don't mind making a run, but I'd kinda like you and Dani to get to know each other.

"You're right of course." She stood and turned, wiping the rail with her napkin. "You only just arrived, and here I am shooing you off. You haven't even seen the property yet."

"I can't wait to see it all." Dani patted his hand and flashed him a smile. "We'll be fine."

Good. About time two of his favorite girls had the chance to get to know one another. "Then it's settled. I'll get a few bags. Text me if there's anything else." He pulled out his keys and made for his SUV.

This weekend was going to be perfect.

Dani waved as Jay left and took another bite of one of Mrs. Hunter's shortbread cookies. Delicious.

"Would you like another dear?"

"No, thank you, but they are wonderful." Buttery and crisp. She could make a meal out of them, but then she'd have trouble fitting into Jay's truck.

"My grandmother's recipe. She never came for a visit without some type of special treat." Mrs. Hunter tapped her fingers against the wicker arm of her chair. "I can't imagine who John is speaking to."

"Jay said he's been sheriff for 23 years straight. Sounds like some type of record." She must be very proud of her husband.

Her warm smile faltered a tad. "It wasn't easy for him to give it up, but necessary."

Dani's alarms went off. He wasn't ill or something, was he? "Why so?" Shoot. That wasn't any of her business. And she had determined to control her thoughtless questions and comments during this trip.

Mrs. Hunter shifted in her seat, scanning the yard from one side to the other. "The time was right, that's all." Her eyes shifted to the right.

Dani internally kicked herself. New topic. "How far along is your daughter? Is it Kristi?"

Mrs. Hunter brightened. "She's officially due in two weeks, but from the looks of her, I can't imagine that she will last that long."

"How exciting." Dani wiped the crumbs from the table and sprinkled them on her plate. She took another sip from her glass.

"Are you interested in having children?" His mother poured herself another glass of lemonade from the chilled pitcher. "Jay's always wanted a big family."

Whoa. Gasping, she kept the lemonade from spewing out her nose but had to cover her mouth to force a swallow before erupting into a fit of coughing.

"Yes." The word was more whisper than voice, but it proved she had airflow.

"I'm so sorry. Are you all right?"

"Yes." She swallowed hard.

"You must come to the baby shower." His mom didn't exactly shift gears but came close. "We've had to put it off for a few weekends, details of life you know, but we're having it on the back patio, rain or shine, next Saturday. You'll come?"

Lemonade burned going down the wrong way. She cleared her throat once more. "I'm afraid I'm scheduled to work next weekend. I'm so sorry."

"No matter. Though I would have loved you getting to meet all of Jay's old friends. He's terribly missed out here."

"That doesn't surprise me one bit. I know you must be very proud of him. Following his father's footsteps, so to speak."

"Oh, we are."

"You have a lovely home." Dani focused on the wind-chimes dangling from a hook over the porch rail. With all of the metal tubes thoroughly tangled in the strings, the chimes swayed in the breeze as a single unit. A shame.

Mrs. Hunter patted her arm and stood. "Are you up for a walk?"

"I'd like that."

Mrs. Hunter glanced down. "Maybe you have

a little country in you after all. You know what shoes to wear." She chuckled. "Let me get my garden boots, and I'll be right back."

Dani touched a single chime, dangling from the knot of all the others. In the breeze of the day, they should be dancing with song. Oh, well.

She wandered to the end of the porch toward the back of the house. Three steps down took her to a stone pathway that led to that covered, outdoor kitchen that would be the venue for the baby shower. Their home was amazing. And fields spread out as far as she could see on all sides.

No, wait, there was a vehicle off in the distance. Must be a road blocked from view by the vegetation. She followed the path to the entertainment area where a wide fireplace formed one corner, and an outdoor kitchen made up an opposite wall. Perfect for parties, the patio contained wrought iron chairs and couches with thick cushions. A fan spun slowly overhead, and even a flat-screened TV hung above the fireplace, thoroughly protected from the elements.

Dani wandered to the far edge where a small fountain that looked like a series of cowboy boots and hats trickled into a broad pond with flicking colors of sunfish swimming around in it. Little treasures hid around every corner.

"You're out of your mind if you think I'm going to stand for this." A man's voice, almost a growl, erupted from somewhere beyond the west wing of the house. A big garage with three open doors took up the end of the broad driveway.

Someone replied, a low timbre, but no words came through.

"You've got your money. Be on your way before I do something you'll regret." Sounded like Mr. Hunter.

She continued the length of the building and stopped at the corner. An old, faded-black SUV sat in front of one of the raised doors on the separate garage. After another wordless rumble, a stocky man in a red baseball cap marched from the open space and climbed into the vehicle.

Mr. Hunter followed and stopped at the doorway. "You heard my answer. You can…." He glanced in her direction. His glare darkened. Wheeling around, he re-entered the building.

Well, she was a delightful house guest. What was she thinking, sneaking around corners? If Mr. Hunter hadn't already disliked her, he sure would now that he'd caught her eavesdropping. Why couldn't she control her curiosity once?

Marji Laine

Chapter Two

Jay hustled down the open highway toward Marseilles. Maybe he shouldn't have left. Kristi and her husband could have picked up chips tomorrow. But no, this was the perfect opportunity for Mom and Dani to bond without him hovering.

If only Dad hadn't been so distracted. He was usually relaxed and funny.

Ten more minutes into little Marseilles, Texas, and he parked in an empty lot at the StopNShop. Used to be the go-to place for a quick trip when he'd lived there, but from the moldy siding and duct-tape repairs on the windows, not so much anymore.

He probably should have gone on to the Super Center on the freeway north of town, but he only needed tortilla chips. Enclosed bags. This place couldn't mess that up, and coming here cut a good 20 minutes off his trip. The urge to check on Dani and Mom became a giant jumping bean in his chest.

"Hunter-man. How the heck are you?"

His high school nickname caught him off guard. Jay wheeled around and stopped short at the sight of his best friend since elementary school walking toward him. "Good to see you, Buddy." He caught him in a half-hug, half-handshake. "Shopping?"

"Here? You gotta be kidding?" Buddy Wills took off his Marseilles Redwings cap with one hand and raked his cropped black hair with the other. "Wouldn't set foot in that vermin asylum."

Jay glanced through the closest window. The guy behind the counter looked vaguely familiar. "That bad?"

His friend leaned closer. "Word is it's a front for pushers."

Arching his eyebrow, Jay studied the place. Was the man kidding? Cops would never allow that, especially not his dad. "Then why are you here?" Bad place for the coach of the high school football team to be.

He laughed. "You know me better than that, Hunter-man. Brews, yes. That other stuff. Huh-uh." He pointed to a neighborhood of clapboard houses behind the building. "Cutting across the parking lot on the way home. The white one with the green shutters. You should come over. Val would love to see you."

Nice place. Good to see they were doing all right. "Thanks, but I only got home a bit ago. Mom sent me on an errand. Needed extra chips. Thought I'd save time and get the items here."

He put a hand on his shoulder. "They do have chips. Depends on how desperate you are."

Was he that desperate? The Super Center

looked better and better.

"Why don't you come to dinner tonight?" Buddy's eyes sparkled.

"Well, my girlfriend—"

"Seriously, y'all have to come. If I tell Valerie I saw you, and she doesn't get to, she'll have my hide."

Hmm. He'd planned to take Dani into town for dinner tonight anyway. "Are you sure?"

Buddy smacked him on the back. "I'm sure I'll get my tail chewed off if you don't. 'Bout seven?"

Jay gave a sharp nod. "Okay. And thanks for the invitation." He shook his hand again and waved as his friend strode toward the little house. Good to see him. Had it really been a year… no two… since Jay had stood beside him as his best man?

He turned his attention again to the convenience store. Only chips. He pushed the glass door, but it stuck. He gave the metal bar a hard shove, forcing the bottom to scrape loudly against his intrusion. Jay didn't know if the workers pushed drugs out of the store, but Buddy was right about its condition. Vermin infested didn't scratch the surface of the dinginess. The man at the counter turned to face him.

Looked familiar, but Jay couldn't quite place him.

Walking to the third aisle, across from the refrigerated selection of beers, he found two bags of tortilla chips and one of cheese curls. Okay, the store didn't even do chips well, but they would have to make these bags work. He collected all three and walked toward the counter.

The clerk eyed him. His initial scowl turned into a smirk. "Got the munchies, cop?"

He would recognize the guy's squirrelly voice anywhere. Dawson Keist. Moody in school, trouble. But then they weren't in school anymore.

"Didn't know you stayed in Marseilles. You still playing guitar?" Though not exactly a band, Dawson and a few others had screeched long into the summer nights. Sometimes, so long that Jay's dad had been dispatched to shut 'em up.

"Tacky's Bar on Fridays." The man punched some buttons on his register. "Not exactly your jam, though. Don't know any Beethoven."

Jay pulled out his wallet. Instead of using his credit card as he'd intended, he withdrew a ten-dollar bill and handed it over. "Glad you get to play."

The man handed over the receipt as he gave a high-pitched laugh.

Someone else came in, blending the screech of the door with Dawson's laughter.

"Well, now. If it isn't the former sheriff's eldest. How nice of you to appear here, in my establishment." The man was shaped like a bullet with stubby legs and thick arms. He shook his head, causing his shaggy, dirty-blond hair to fall into his eyes. "Boy, you are the spitting image of your old man."

Boy? Might as well have used a curse word or called him a half-breed. Especially since their coloring was the only resemblance they shared.

The man looked from Jay's toes to his eyes. "Only you're not in miniature like the ex-sheriff."

Really? The man had no room to talk. "Okay." Time to make his way out before he really got ticked off.

Bullet-man stood in front of the door like a cinder block and made no move to give room for Jay to leave. "I have a message for your folks."

Jay definitely should have gone to the Super Center. "They both have cell phones. Why don't you call them?"

"Tell your dad that I'll only do business with your mom from now on." His mouth spread into what was probably supposed to be a leer. "She's much nicer."

"I'm not a messenger service." He'd had enough of this creep. He stepped around him toward the entrance.

"Now, hold on, boy." The guy took hold of Jay's arm.

Big mistake.

Jay dropped his sack and pivoted around the man, taking his hand halfway up his back. "I'm not your boy."

The man let out a yell. Dawson made a move to come out from behind the counter, but Jay pulled the man's arm higher. "Tell your cashier to stay."

"Get back, Keist." The man practically screamed.

Jay eased tension on his arm and pulled him backward. His sack was only a foot away, but he couldn't keep hold of the store owner and retrieve it at the same time. He could wedge the door open with his foot, though. "You really need to get this door fixed."

He shoved the guy forward, grabbed his bag, and ducked out of the store. Sprinting for his truck, he had to veer around an older model, black SUV, but he kept his head down in case either of the two were armed. Jumping into his seat, he jammed his key into the ignition and peeled out of the gravel lot onto Cannon Street. Thankfully, neither of the men chose to follow.

Good thing. He opened his console and checked his weapon. He would have hated to use that again. His last shot had been a fatal one. His first fatal one. He wasn't keen on reliving the experience of looking down the short barrel at another human being.

What were mom and dad thinking, doing business with someone like him? What kind of business could they possibly have?

Dani made her way back across the patio.

"There you are." Mrs. Hunter, wearing pink and purple rain boots, came from the back door. "Ready for a short walk?" She urged Dani toward a brick walkway.

"You must do a lot of entertaining."

"We enjoy opening up for friends and family. That's how the Fourth Party started out. Even before we moved here, we filled our house and backyard with as many folks as could come."

"What fun." Dani followed her to a tall, metal gate separating the sculptured backyard from a close-cropped field. Farther from the house, the gale from the front yard caught Dani's hair and whipped it into knots.

Mrs. Hunter stopped and fiddled with a latch before pushing the gate open. "This is one of the things we love about our ranch."

"The fence?" Why was a fence all that great?

She chuckled. "Seems like such a silly thing, but the people who built this ranch did so exactly the way we would have. A few cows. Maybe someday, we'll get a couple of horses for the grandkids."

"Jay mentioned you had cows."

"They're somewhere around here. Grass-fed. Annoying bullies, but we get the last laugh."

What was there to laugh about? "Do you have fresh milk?"

"Oh, no. Too much trouble to do the dairy stuff, but the beef is delicious."

Dani stumbled. "You eat your cows?"

"They're a little big for pets, dear." Mrs. Hunter led her around a small pond with trees on the opposite side. Near the trees, three white-faced cows grazed.

"They look so sweet."

The woman laughed again. "Don't let Jay hear you say that. Jay used to help my father with his cattle. One time, he bent down too close to a calf. The ornery thing tried to take a bite out of his hair. Pulled out a shock of it, if I remember correctly."

"Ow. So he's not a fan of cows."

"Not like he's a fan of beef." Her eyes sparkled.

Dani had seen his penchant for steak first hand.

"Things are different on a ranch." Jay's mom went on about cows and chickens. Dani smiled and nodded and tried to keep her responses from showing her incompetence in that area.

So Jay was a real farm boy. He'd mentioned rodeo before. Hard to believe her super-suave, put-together crime scene supervisor had roots like this. He looked more like a successful business executive than a cop most of the time.

Mrs. Hunter continued explaining about the ranch. She practically glowed. "This is what I've always wanted. I had a little flower bed in town, but room to really plant and raise cattle... it's a dream."

"Does your youngest help out?" Jay said his little brother still lived here with his parents.

"He's not quite as... enthusiastic as John and I are. Kyle moved in with us last year. His marriage broke up after he had trouble finding a job in Houston."

"I'm so sorry. I didn't know."

Mrs. Hunter's pace became more of a stomp. "His wife considered him charmingly small-town. That charm held out for less than two years before she was ready to move on. The fact that he wanted to move home, back to 'the sticks' as she called this town, sealed her decision to divorce him."

Shoot. Dani hadn't intended to pry into anything, only wanted to keep Mrs. Hunter talking. "What a blessing that he could come home to you." At least he'd had people who cared about him to support him through the disaster.

"Yes, but you'll understand if Kyle's experience with his city girl has made me slightly gun-shy."

Oh, great. Mrs. Hunter didn't have to expound further. Plainly she was concerned about Dani and Jay's relationship. "I really care about your son." She couldn't help it if she'd killed a cactus, sneezed around most animals, and usually only cooked frozen dinners and boxed macaroni and cheese. She loved the man, even if she hadn't been able to tell him.

Not that she held out much hope for their relationship. Their pasts were so different.

Mrs. Hunter paused at another gate and faced Dani. "I believe you. And from hearing about the experiences the two of you have had together, I don't think you'd ever want to intentionally hurt him."

"But you think I will?" Agh. Why couldn't she let comments like that go without having to pursue them?

The woman pulled open the next gate and ushered Dani through. "Frankly, dear, my hope is that you'll only break his heart."

Strange. If only Dani could assure her that she would never do that. Would do her ultimate to make Jay happy.

But reality shattered that fantasy.

"Shame on me." Mrs. Hunter slapped the back of her hand. "We're only just getting to know each other, and I'm letting all of my worries spill over. Please forgive me."

"Absolutely." She still felt a little foggy on the *worries* of which Mrs. Hunter spoke.

"I'm glad to have finally met the woman of whom my son speaks so fondly." She took Dani's hand. "He does, you know."

Dani pulled a tendril behind her ear and tried to reduce the grin that begged to spread. "That's sweet." The grin was winning out.

His mom drew her forward to where a small building, like an outhouse, marked a corner of a large field. "This is my pride and joy."

A huge square garden, about the width of a football field, spread out. Had Dani been walking through Peru, she wouldn't have felt any less out of her element. She recognized something that might have been corn stalks but only determined that from TV commercials. "What all do you have here?"

"Tomatoes over there. Already had a nice crop of those, and melons. You'll have some at the party."

Looked like some sort of bean hung off a row of plants. Another row had bushes. In fact, every raised furrow showed signs of greenery. "You do all of this yourself?"

Mrs. Hunter didn't reply. She gazed in the

direction of the road Dani had noticed before.

A couple of cars had stopped. Didn't look like an accident, but from that distance she wouldn't have heard any squeal of tires or clash of metal. One person stood by an old tan truck. Three others climbed from something blocked by a clump of cottonwood trees. The one in the truck turned and ran, but one of the others caught him and punched him.

"Oh, no." Mrs. Hunter ran for the garden gate, tugged it open, and took off at a trot the way they'd come.

Dani followed her toward the house. "Should we call the police?" She caught up with Mrs. Hunter and huffed out her question.

The older lady slowed, breathing hard. "Won't come out here. Sheriff's a… he won't come either." She blew out a long exhale and began jogging again.

Dani eyed the cows that had come a little closer, but they didn't seem to mind or even acknowledge the ladies running across their dinner table.

Mrs. Hunter stopped again at the front gate and unlatched it. She was struggling to catch her breath at this point and paused with her hands on her knees.

"Are you all right?"

"Close that…." She pointed at the metal bars that Dani had come through.

Dani whirled around and latched the pieces together, then returned to the woman. "Who are those people?"

"My keys… hook by… back door." She straightened and moved toward the garage.

"I'll get them." Dani darted into the house and found a hook board beside the door. Three different sets of keys hung there. She grabbed them all. Hopefully she wasn't marooning anyone.

By the time she'd reached the garage, Mrs. Hunter was fully composed and in the driver's seat of her sedan.

Without invitation, Dani climbed in and held out all three fobs. Taking one, the woman started the engine and backed out of the large building.

"Did you tell Mr. Hunter?" He'd been in the garage last time she'd seen him.

"He's probably up to the house." She turned the car around in the grass. "Hold on, dear."

Dani fastened her seatbelt. "Who was out there?"

"Can't be sure about that. We could hardly see them."

There was something hollow in her response. But then maybe her kindness poured from a sympathetic heart. Silence filled the car as Mrs. Hunter barreled down the highway. The woman was stiff as a flagpole. She turned right onto a one-lane road that weaved through a pine-filled forest.

Dani struggled to stay in her seat and clutched the hand-hold built into the passenger doorway.

Mrs. Hunter paused at the asphalt entrance to a highway and turned right again. "This is the place."

No sign of any cars or people, beaten up or otherwise. Mrs. Hunter halted and shoved the Toyota into park.

Climbing from her seat, Dani scanned the ground, then wandered over to the grassy area next to the asphalt. One of the vehicles had pulled off the road. That didn't seem like a chance meeting. Some boot prints in the soft shoulder ended in an area where the dirt had been disrupted and little divots covered the surface. "Looks like they scuffled here."

Mrs. Hunter didn't answer. She spun toward the sound of an oncoming vehicle fast-approaching from the bend.

Marji Laine

Chapter Three

Jay spotted his mom and Dani on the side of the road. Both had wary eyes and flattened mouths. Well, that didn't look good. Surely Mom hadn't stirred up an argument, had she? She had a gift of counseling and an irritating habit of helping people pick at their emotional scabs until the whole story blurted out.

Knowing Dani as well as he did, she wouldn't welcome his mom's prying.

He climbed from the truck. "Everything okay?" He glanced from his mother's worried face to Dani's relieved one.

His girl heaved a huge sigh. "Thought you might be a group of thugs."

What was she talking about? "Why are y'all out here?"

"Nothing of consequence." Mom waved it off like a fly. "Merely a car that had stopped. We thought they might need help."

Dani's eyes widened, and she stared at his mom.

Mom waved at the invisible insect again and moved to her car. "I guess I can let you two find your own way back to the ranch." She paused and winked at Dani. "I did enjoy our chat, dear, and I am glad you're here."

Dani's mouth hung open for a second, then she seemed to compose herself. "Uh, thanks for the tour. I loved your garden." She gave a brief wave before touching her finger to her chin. She turned to Jay. "You really were a farm boy, huh?"

"I worked at Grandpa's place until I moved away after high school." He eyed his mom as she urged the car back onto the asphalt. "You going to tell me why my mom was lying to me?" Though usually honest, she and Dad both tried to protect him and his siblings from time to time. What could he possibly need protection from this time? Unless it had something to do with Dani?

"I…." She shook her head slowly. "I seriously have no idea."

"What were y'all doing out here?"

"We were in your mom's garden." She shielded her eyes. "Over there?"

"Yeah, up on the hill. See the spring house?" Most people thought it to be an old outhouse. "It pumps water for the garden from an underground spring."

"Oh, that's what that is."

"And?" He leaned back on the grill of his truck. No hurry. He'd wait all afternoon for the full story.

"It wasn't that big a deal. A truck and some other vehicle stopped out here. Three or four guys were walking around."

"All men?"

She shrugged. "I thought so, but you see how far it is, and there were trees in the way. Anyway, they ganged-up on one of the guys." She walked a few feet away and pointed to the ground. "I think they were fighting here."

Looked like it from the scraped earth.

Pausing, she knelt and brushed away a broken bush. "Is this someone's brake light?"

He joined her. Sure enough, little chunks of red plastic were in and around the weeds that lined that part of the road.

"The truck was here. See the tire prints?"

"Good eyes." He grinned at her. "Beautiful eyes as well." He reached for her, and she rose into his arms and rested her hands against his chest.

"You and Mom have a nice chat?"

"Sure. She's very nice." Her gaze drifted to somewhere around the collar of his shirt. "Very proud of you."

The worry-wrinkle that formed between

Dani's brows told him there was more. "Something's bothering you."

"It's only that…." She toyed with the collar of his tee shirt, then tilted her head and looked over his shoulder. "Your mom loves you very much."

Jay gave her a sidelong look. "And?"

"I get the feeling she's a little wary of me." Lifting her warm, brown eyes to his face allowed a tear to escape and drip onto her smooth cheek. "She doesn't want to see you hurt, and neither do I."

He brushed her tear into her hairline. "That makes three of us." He pressed a kiss to her forehead. He'd have to talk to Mom. Help her realize the depth of his feelings for Dani. Once she understood, her worrywart would fade.

She wrapped her hands around his back and laid her head against his chest. Exactly the way he loved to hold her.

"Honey, don't think about what my mom said. My brother, Kyle, had a bad time with his wife. Married her quick and against wise counsel and flat-out common sense. Mom blames the two worlds in which they lived."

"She told me a little of that. And I am a city girl, too."

"Yeah, but I'm a city guy, now. I love both places, but I left Marseilles a long time ago." He laid his cheek against her soft hair. "I chose Dallas. Mom didn't like it, but she's learned to respect my decision. I guess she's always hoped I'd come back here, but I won't. Dallas is where I'll stay. Especially since you're there."

She released a short breath. "Oh, Jay. I don't deserve you."

He chuckled. Sounded like he'd finally gotten through to her. Hopefully it wouldn't be too long before he'd hear the three precious words given back to him, but chances were, that declaration would take her a bit longer. Whether from a painful past relationship or a natural guardedness, Dani wasn't apt to give that declaration unless it was with no reservations. "Let me get you back to the ranch. We're going to dinner tonight with an old friend of mine and his wife."

She stepped back and stared at him. "More new people?"

"Funny, sweet, and they'll tell you all sorts of goofy stories about me." He winked. That ought to make her feel better.

"Oh, well, if I'm going to get the insight on Sergeant Jay Hunter, then I'm all in." She grinned.

That was certainly the goal. He opened the door for her, then strode around the front and climbed in on his own side.

"What about the fight and stuff?" She stared at the ground. "It sure upset your mom."

He had his suspicions about that as well. "You said it was a truck?"

"Yeah, sort of tan. Older model."

Jay clenched his jaw. Kyle. "I hope I'm wrong about this, but I bet Mom thought it was my brother." He had only barely gotten onto the highway before his brother's truck shot past.

"That was the one I saw." Dani pointed through the windshield.

"Thought so. If it's all right with you, I'd like to have a talk with him before we leave for dinner." He accelerated, but catching his brother was next to impossible.

"No wonder your mom was so upset."

"It's not the first time he's had a run-in with the wrong type of people." He glanced at her. "And, yes, sometimes the wrong types of people are even hanging out in little backwoods towns like Marseilles."

"Hard to believe." She settled back in her seat. "I know he couldn't find a job in Houston, but is he having other problems?"

Kyle *was* a problem. From the moment he fell in love with a woman whose character was as shallow as mom's bird feeder. "I haven't been around much lately. Obviously. But he's always been a hothead. And stubborn, you know what I mean?"

"Yeah." She lapsed into silence.

He shouldn't have said anything. "I don't want you to assume the worst. He was a good kid. Fun and spontaneous. Only recently...."

"I understand."

Did she? He didn't. Not completely. He swallowed the anger he thought he'd dealt with long ago. A little over a year ago, to be exact. Though his dad had never completely explained his reasons for retiring from the sheriff's department, Kyle had just moved home. No such thing as coincidence to Jay's way of thinking. "He has a talent for listening to wise advice and doing the direct opposite."

"That's true of a lot of young people, though. Isn't it."

He tilted his head. Hard to argue with her truth. He pulled into the driveway and parked behind the truck. His brother had left the windows down like he always had in the past. More than one storm had soaked the interior. Jay glanced at the sky. Nothing like that today.

"Broken tail lights." Dani had emerged from the truck before he could get all the way around to her. She stopped at the back of Kyle's Toyota. "Both of them. That's not an accident."

He scanned the bed of the truck. Nothing out of the ordinary. Reaching the driver's door, he pulled it open.

"Don't you need a warrant for a search?"

He glanced at her smirk and cracked a smile. She could always make him feel better. "Just rolling up the windows. Hopefully, I won't find anything that would… warrant a warrant." He winked.

"Hardy-Har." She went to the other side and climbed in to reach the broken crank.

He examined some of the junk that had found its way between the seats—cans, fast food bags, wrappers of all sorts, along with three work gloves, a pitching wedge, and a broken baseball bat. "Looks like he's been hauling junk. But nothing that would be worth beating anyone up."

"I didn't say he was doing the beating, Jay." She touched his shoulder, and he turned toward her. "The guy in this truck was the one getting punched. And here's some proof." She pointed to a smear of what might have been blood on the torn seat cover beside his knee.

And here Jay was believing the worst about his own brother. "I better talk to him."

Dani scooted backward. "Oh…." She knocked a Styrofoam cup from the dashboard holder. Soda spilled over her arm and onto the floor. "I'm so sorry."

"Ha. You're the one who got the sticky bath. Stale Dr Pepper, I bet." He handed her some of the napkins from a bag between the seats.

"But I got it all over."

"I promise. This truck has seen worse." Much worse. He leaned over to pick up the empty cup and halted. Great. Jay ground his back teeth together and picked up the tiny bag that had been lying under the cup. White powder filled it. "Did you see this?"

"Oh, no. That's not...."

Jay slammed his palm against the steering wheel. With everything else, now the boy had to get involved with drugs. He climbed out.

"Maybe that's why they were beating him?" She struggled out and shut the door, but she stopped him as he rounded the front of the car. "You need to chill before you go in there."

"What was Kyle thinking?" Jay practically growled.

"If you want to find out..." A worried pucker formed between her brows. "...listen to him more than you talk."

He blew out a long exhale. Too bad expelling his anger wasn't so easy.

"He's your brother. Let him know how much you care about him." She planted a kiss on his nose.

He nodded, still kneading the enamel off his molars. He led her through the front door.

"I'll find my way." Dani veered off toward the

family room.

Jay glanced up the stairs. What was he going to say? Something without shouting, preferably. *God, give me some words.* He hadn't even seen Kyle since Christmas. He paused at his brother's closed door and took a full breath. He didn't need words. He needed patience. *Help me listen.* Like Dani had suggested.

He knocked.

Kyle didn't answer the door. Maybe he was downstairs with Mom and Dad.

Jay knocked again.

"What." No question to the word, merely a challenge.

"It's Jay."

"I'll be down in a while."

No greeting or welcome home. Something was definitely wrong, and Jay wasn't about to leave. Especially not with what had looked like an ounce of cocaine in his pocket. "I need to talk with you."

"Can't it wait?"

Enough of this. Jay turned the knob and pushed the door open.

"Hey. My room. My privacy." His brother, shirtless, turned his back and went into the adjoining bathroom.

The room wasn't the mess he'd expected. Maybe that was what the truck was for. A tee shirt lay crumpled on the floor, smeared with what had to be blood. A lot of it.

Jay picked up the shirt. "Who beat you up?"

"What are you talking about?" Kyle turned on the water in the sink.

Jay stepped into the wide bathroom before he could get locked out of it. "This." He held up the shirt. "Dani saw part of the fight."

"That's right. You brought your girl home to meet the folks." His brother turned his back toward Jay.

"Didn't answer my question." Jay held his ground. "And Mom saw the fight, too."

Kyle turned around. Though he was the

spitting image of his dad, an ugly cut above his black eyes seeped blood and spoiled the similarity. His nose had dried blood under it and a purplish bruise on one side. Likely broken. His thickened bottom lip also bled. "Mom saw me get hit? Aw, man."

Jay recoiled at his brother's face. His hands fisted at his sides. "Who did this?"

"I can't get the bleeding to stop." Kyle held out a reddened washrag and sat on the lid of the toilet.

Jay swallowed his protection mode and scanned his brother's wound. "Needs stitches." He took the rag and pressed the edges of the cut together.

"Mom's gonna kill me."

"Not for getting beat up, she won't. Unless you get your blood all over her carpet." Jay's attempt at levity was as much to calm him down as to engage his brother. "Why would someone do this?"

Kyle shrugged and opened a first aid kit on the counter. "I found this."

Jay eyed the contents. The butterfly bandages would help. "You gonna tell me or not?" He wet some gauze with peroxide and dabbed it onto the wound.

"Ow. What are you doing to me?"

Wiping away a drip of the bubbling liquid, Jay dried the area around the cut with another piece of gauze. "Getting things cleaned." He applied a piece of the special tape across the middle of the cut which pressed the edges together. "Gonna make a bad scar if you don't get stitches."

"I'll chance it."

He added two more butterfly strips. They didn't completely stop the bleeding, but they helped. "Needs some ice." He taped another piece of gauze across the wound.

"I can't go downstairs. Not like this."

"Put on a shirt." Jay was only half serious. "But really, before Dad tries to go after whoever did this, suppose you tell me what's going on."

"Just some guys. Not part of my fan club."

"Obviously. There a reason they decided to decorate today?"

He shrugged. "Been helping out at the feed store. With the silos. You know. Got a call from one of the guys on the job with me this morning that he found my wallet. Wanted to bring it to me."

"And they ambushed you when you met him? Who was this guy?"

"Doesn't matter. Someone who doesn't like me much, but I did get my wallet back."

"Your face isn't a tradable commodity. Did you call the sheriff?"

He scoffed. "Heck, no."

Probably because of what he was hiding in his truck. The cocaine packet burned a hole in Jay's pocket.

"Listen, big brother, I know you want to defend me, but getting you involved will only make matters worse."

Jay leaned back against the open door and stared at his brother. "Worse? Like this." Jay held up the packet of powder. Hopefully, his brother would level with him and not make up some lame excuse.

Kyle's gaze didn't waver or even change. "What is that?"

"I think it's cocaine. And I got it from your truck."

His un-swollen eye squinted. "No, you did not. I didn't have anything like that in my truck or anywhere else." He stood and pushed out of the bathroom.

So far, his reaction hadn't shown any defensiveness whatsoever.

His brother halted, a clean shirt halfway up his arms. "And just what were you doing searching my truck?"

"I was rolling up the windows. Dani knocked over your drink. She's a little on the clumsy side sometimes."

"And you happened to find it?" He finished putting on the shirt and crossed his arms.

"It was in the cup-holder. Stupid hiding place, by the way. If a cop suspects driving under the influence, the first thing he'll do is to check a cup for liquor."

"Thanks for the lesson." He yanked his dirty tee shirt from Jay's hand and went back into the bathroom, shoving it into the sink.

Dani's words flowed back over his exasperation. *Listen. Don't talk.* "So about this packet?"

Jay let the silence broaden and watched his brother scrub at the stains on his shirt for a few minutes.

Finally, Kyle faced him. "I've never seen that before. I have no idea what it is or where it came from." Seemed earnest.

"Then you won't mind if I do this?" Jay lifted the lid of the toilet and eyed his brother.

Kyle had turned back to his shirt. He punched the plug and let the water gurgle out. "Be my guest." He wrung out his shirt. "I guess it doesn't matter if Mom notices the stains since she saw the fight."

No reaction from Kyle. He really *didn't* care. "Yeah. She and Dani were in the garden." Jay let the packet fall and flushed the lever, keeping Kyle in view.

Rolling his shirt into a tight ball, he didn't even flinch. He carried the dirty thing to a hamper on the back of his door. "Still not going to go downstairs. This face would freak Mom out bigtime. And wouldn't be a great way to meet the girl who might be my new sister, right?" He winced when his smile hit his torn lip. "Might need two ice packs."

Jay clapped his palm on his shoulder. "I'm on it."

"And some dinner?"

"That one I'll leave to Mom." He paused at the doorway. "She'll be okay, Kyle. And you still need stitches."

"We'll see." He tossed the towel into the hamper. "Hey. Good to have you home, you big ole' bear."

Jay smiled at the childhood moniker. "Good to be here, man cub." He closed the door but paused. Either Kyle was a much better actor than Jay had ever noticed before, or someone else had put the packet in his car.

If that was so, then who? And why?

Chapter Four

City girl.

Dani raced up to the house, her pounding heart drowning out the frustration in her wake. How could she have been so stupid?

She blasted through the kitchen door and ran directly into Jay, who carried a couple of blue ice packs.

"Whoa, looks like you must have seen one of the snakes that hang around the pond." He set the packs down on the counter.

Visiting snakes would have been easier to deal with. "Take me home."

His mouth dropped open, and he laid his fingertips against her upper arms. "Sweetheart, what happened?"

Stupid idiocy happened. "I…." She gasped a breath and spat it out. "I left the garden gate open."

The look of concern in his eyes faded into realization. "Oh, no. The cows?"

She nodded, fighting tears. "Those neat little furrows your mom was so proud of look like dirt bikers had a rally."

His eyes shut. "Oh, honey." When he opened them again, he bent toward her and peered into hers. "This was an accident."

"She hates me. And for good reason."

"She's only upset right now. She'll be okay." He kissed the top of her head. "Go on out to my truck. I'll smooth things over with Mom and Dad."

Mrs. Hunter's voice neared. "My limas and black eyes. Even the cucumbers. They were almost ready…."

Dani darted for the front door, collecting her

purse on the way past the coat rack. Utter failure. The woman had been so kind to her. And how does she repay? By destroying her *pride and joy*.

She leaned against the back of Jay's truck and looked out onto the small lake. Some big bird waded near the edge of it. Spreading outlandishly wide wings, the creature pumped them twice, then lifted into the air.

If only she could do something similar. But then where could she go? Matthew had given her strict orders not to return to Dallas until he contacted her. She pulled her phone from her purse and scanned for a message she knew wasn't there. She toyed with calling the man, but that never went well. And he wasn't one to sympathize with her mistakes.

Jay joined her after a few minutes. "Mom is gonna be fine."

"I made your father mad, too. I overheard him yelling at someone, and he caught me eavesdropping."

Marji Laine

He opened her door and helped her inside. "He'll get over that. And you can't help that you're so observant."

"Ha. So much so that I didn't register why your mom was so careful about re-latching the gates as we went through them." Fat lotta good her skills did her.

Her eyes stung as she swung her gaze up to Jay when he climbed in next to her. "I'm so sorry. I didn't even think."

"Honey, it's all right. Mom will cool off. She's not nearly as angry at you as she is at her own forgetfulness." He kissed her temple. "Said so herself."

"She hates me. And for good reason."

"I actually think she likes you. Quite a lot."

"Except she has concerns. And after what happened to your brother, she has good reason." Dani remained quiet until they reached the end of the drive. "I'm not sure this trip was such a great idea."

"Rocky start, agreed." He turned left onto the highway. "My fault, though. I hit Mom and Dad with this at the last minute." He turned in the opposite direction from the way they had come. "They'll be fine by the time we finish dinner. And you'll get a chance to meet a couple of my closest friends."

"Dinner. Oh, shoot." His mention of that hadn't gone anywhere near her brain. She beat dust from her jeans. "Oh, Jay, I'm not presentable for a dinner party. I walked all over your folks' property. Probably smell like a middle school gym."

"Ha. You're beautiful. You're always beautiful, and my friends will enjoy meeting you." He paused at a stop sign and smiled at her with that handsome grin of his.

"Are you sure I'm not way under-dressed? I don't want to mess up anymore." She was already on iffy ground with his parents.

He squeezed her hand. "We all mess up. But God is good."

He had her with that.

"You'll have fun getting to know Buddy and Valerie." Slowing to the crawl that was the posted speed limit, Jay eased into the outskirts of a little town. "And, I'm sure by tomorrow, Mom and Dad will be back to normal."

"But I'll still be myself." And that was the real problem.

He chuckled. "Beautiful, kind, funny, smart."

"Stop." She flicked her hand down in a mock show of resistance.

He chuckled. "Welcome to Marseilles." He pronounced it like the name Mar-cee, though the sign at the city limits clearly had it in the traditional French spelling.

"That's still a weird way to say the name."

He winked. "Not weird. Texanized. We tend to claim our towns with our drawl. Like It-lee instead of Italy and Cor-*inth* instead of *Cor*-inth. I'm surprised the founders didn't pronounce Paris, Texas in a special way."

"Like what? Pareees?"

"Something like that." He turned onto a square.

Charming, with an old, limestone library in a center lot and cute storefronts surrounding the building. "Do you get a lot of downtown shoppers?"

"Actually, yes, we're known for antiques, but there are several nice shops of all sorts down here. Even get a year-round tourist trade for some of the specialty stores."

She'd have to investigate further—a non-criminal investigation for a change. What a concept.

"Buddy and I have known each other since grade school. He and Valerie were high school sweethearts." He pulled up to a little white house, a single story probably built in the twenties with a wide front porch and forest green shutters.

"If they're friends of yours, they're friends of mine." She choked on the cliché, as Jay wrinkled his nose.

The truth was, her liking *them* wasn't the problem. Would they like her?

Jay helped her out and led her up the steps.

Butterflies erupted all through her stomach as he knocked. She paused on the stairs behind him and forced herself to breathe. She had to make a good impression this time. If by some slim chance Jay still loved her after he learned her history, she needed to be able to get along with the people who were important to him. She braced herself and applied her most glowing smile.

The door opened. "Jay Hunter." A Barbie doll stepped directly into Jay's arms and planted a kiss right on his lips.

What in the....

Jay pulled back and gazed at his old flame. She was still a knockout. "Lauren. What are you doing here?"

"Surprising you." She leaned in and caught

him in an embrace. "Valerie invited me." She released him and let her baby blues pierce him. "High time we got together and chatted about the old days. Who knows? Maybe we can get together again in other ways." Her gaze turned seductive and lingered for a moment before she reentered the house.

His mouth hung opened. Dani joined him at the door. She wrapped her fingers around his hand, waking him from his dumbfounded state. He looked down at the question on her face, the raised eyebrow and pursed lips. Shaking his head, he gave a slight shrug. No way he'd encourage the woman, but she didn't seem to need much encouragement.

She faced the door as though it were a firing squad. "Maybe this wasn't such a great idea."

"I don't understand. I told Buddy I was bringing you." Hadn't his friend heard him?

"Well, come on. Come in, sugar." Lauren chuckled in a low, sultry voice. "Told you I'd shock him."

He stepped inside to see Valerie's smiling face. "I'm so glad Buddy ran into you, today."

Dani hung back. "This is a little awkward." He pushed the door fully open. She had no choice but to join him. She looked like she wanted nothing except escape. He couldn't blame her. After this weekend, she might never even speak to him again. "I wanted to introduce you to my girlfriend, Dani Foster."

Lauren's half-opened eyelids opened fully, and her smile froze in place. "Oh, dear. Well, this is embarrassing."

Valerie lurched forward. "Buddy!" She reached out her hand to Dani. "I am so sorry for the ambush. I had no idea."

"Well, hey, Hunter-man." Buddy came from what must've been the kitchen and whacked Jay on the back. "Lauren. Hi. Didn't know you'd be here."

Valerie jutted her pointed chin toward her husband. "Why didn't you tell me that Jay was bringing his girlfriend?" She whispered the question, but in the awkward silence, no one could have missed her words.

"I didn't mention it? My bad." Buddy wiped his hand down his black apron and held it out to Dani. "You must be the charming plus-one he mentioned."

"Dani. Dani Foster." She flashed a brilliant smile at her host. "Thank you so much for the invitation."

Jay stared in awe at his girl. Not only did she engage Bud and Val, but she approached Lauren, as well.

The blond hadn't changed much since high school. Still slender, almost too skinny, tall, and practically perfect. She stuck out a stiff hand toward Dani. "So nice to meet you." Lauren backed toward the door, as stiff as the painted grin on her face. "I'm going to just go on, now."

"Nonsense." Buddy stepped over and blocked her way. "Nothing says a bunch of old friends…" He glanced at Dani. "…and a charming new one can't have dinner and a few laughs."

Buddy could charm the readers off of the church secretary and the school librarian in the same day.

"Well, I guess." Lauren looked toward Jay.

Though he'd rather see her leave, he couldn't be rude. He smiled. "Buddy's right. Friends having dinner." Dani smiled up at him. Okay, this could still work out all right and give Dani a crazy event to remember.

Valerie opened the china cabinet that spanned one wall of her living/dining room. "Honey, you should check on the ribs."

"Ribs? You did barbecue?" Ha. Buddy couldn't even scramble eggs.

"Let me show you the grill." He walked through a swinging door.

Jay held onto Dani's hand. With her feeling so raw, he wasn't about to leave her alone.

"We won't bite her, Jay." Valerie gave him a nudge into the kitchen. "Through that door to the back." She pointed.

Had this been a mistake? He leaned his head back to work out the kinks in his tense muscles.

"I'm fine, Jay." Dani released his hand.

Well, if she was sure. He followed the direction to find Buddy in his backyard and was greeted by a shaggy, cream-colored giant. "What is this?" He laughed as he caught a lick on his chin.

"Down, Pookie."

"Pookie?" Oh, no. His dear old friend had become a… a husband. "You're gonna have to give up a man-card for uttering that wimpy dog name."

"I know, right?" Buddy chuckled. "She was nothing but a tiny ball of fluff when I got her for Valerie last year. Had no idea she'd get so big. Mutt. No clue of the type, but something big. Maybe a great Dane mix?"

"Or St. Bernard." Jay patted the dog's head. "A shame she doesn't answer to something like *Horse* or *Ox*."

"I ought to try to pin one of those on her." He

opened the shiny lid of a large grill. "My new baby."

"Nice." Jay listened with half an ear to the grill's attributes. Not really his thing, but he made appropriate responses and let his friend talk himself out.

"And it looks like these are ready." Buddy cut into one of the pieces of meat. "Your girl like ribs?"

Jay had no idea. "I guess we'll both find out."

"Hey, man. Sorry about the mix up." He handed Jay a plate and started loading it with racks of ribs. "Val would never have invited Lauren if she'd known about Dani. My bad for forgetting that part."

"Not a problem. Dani's grace itself." And he could hope that she'd have a good time in spite of the discomfort. It wouldn't have been any better if they'd stayed at the ranch. Especially with Mom and Dad's issues. And Kyle's.

Good grief, no wonder Dani wanted to leave.

Chapter Five

Despite her confidence in urging Jay to visit with his friend, Dani's knees felt like noodles. These people had known him all of his life. And intimately, or so it seemed. She followed the women into the kitchen where she volunteered to rinse the salad makings. Something for her hands to do.

Valerie shoved her long tan-ish braids aside and cut into a pineapple. "So how long have you known Jay?"

"Only a few months." Actually closer to a year, but their almost-six months of dating had been constantly interrupted.

Lauren, a platinum blonde, drifted to the sink to rinse some strawberries. "How long have we known him, Val?"

"Ha, since birth. Well, mine anyway. Our parents have been friends forever. He used to pour sand on my head when we'd go to a family camp out on the lake." Her perfect white teeth were even more bright, set off by her smooth, light brown complexion.

"Not Jay. Mr. Perfect?" Lauren's laugh was a jingling of silver bells. "I can't even imagine him being so mean."

Valerie started chunking the pineapple and letting it drop into a bowl. "Not mean. He was trying to build a crown on my head."

"Ah. So he's always been Prince Charming. I met him in eighth grade history with Mr. Ritchie. He was adorable then, too."

If Lauren kept gushing, she'd need to start rationing. After all, it was July. Dani smirked at her own pun but kept her focus on the romaine leaves.

"I wouldn't say adorable. He decided we both needed mustaches when we were eight. Only he used a permanent marker. He got compliments. I got teased for over a week until the remainders of the stain finally faded."

A laugh escaped. So he'd been a scamp. Dani would be sure to tease him about that, later.

Lauren glanced at her. "So how do you like his mom and dad? Caroline and I used to have the most fun working in her garden together. With all that land, I'll bet she has a full-fledged farm now."

Oh great, another gardener. "They're very nice. Mrs. Hunter showed me her garden. She does seem to be a master."

"There's something about digging into the soil. Making things grow. Such a feeling of power when the produce is as beautiful as you imagined it would be." Lauren added washed blueberries to the strawberries that she'd rinsed.

"Do you still garden?" Maybe if Dani got her

talking about her passion, she wouldn't ask too many questions.

"Not anymore." A frown marred the doll's perfect face. "My high-rise apartment faces north."

Ah. No direct sunlight. *See, I know something about gardening.*

"What do you do for fun, Dani?" Valerie poured her pineapple in with Lauren's fruit.

Fun. Well, she couldn't mention the photography that she used to enjoy, or singing in her church choir.

"Grab the dressings from the fridge, Lauren." Valerie picked up the fruit salad. "Can you bring in the romaine?"

"Sure." Dani followed her to the table and set her green salad next to the other bowl.

Lauren set the dressings next to it. "Let's sit down and wait for the fellows."

"Yes, I'll be right back." Valerie scampered back into the kitchen.

Meanwhile, the blonde model of perfection in

lace-covered white pants and a navy silk tank practically hovered over the floor like some sort of elegant cloud. Something blue sparkled from around her neck and even her hoop earrings had blue and white sparkles. More than a little overdressed for a simple dinner party. Valerie, though stylish with her numerous thin braids, wore Capris and a tee shirt. Dani looked down at her comfortable jeans and slightly wrinkled blouse. If only she'd had a chance to change.

"You are a lucky lady, Dani. Jay is certainly a prize." Lauren lowered herself to the cushion beside Dani. "I can't believe I let such a man go, but stupidity and youth go hand in hand."

"Yeah." Valerie set a variety of salad additions on the table, then joined them and sat in a wingback. "I actually broke up with Buddy a few years after high school. No good reason except that I'd never gone out with anyone else. Thought I should have some other experiences. Only took a week to realize what a mistake that was."

"Wish I'd have learned my lesson that fast. Then Jay and I would likely be living across the street from y'all." She smiled at Dani. "But I guess I just have to lick my wounds. Huh."

Yes, you do. Dani mustered a smile. "What was it like growing up in such a small town? I've only lived in large cities."

"Oh, well. Everyone is into everyone else's business. In fact, if you don't know what rumor is being spread around town, it probably involves you." Lauren let out another trickle of perfect laughter. She and Valerie began a new discussion, this one about their school friends who had moved away. The men returned, broadening the topic to new people as they sat at the dinner table. After the prayer, the conversation ebbed when everyone started eating.

Having never tried ribs before, Dani watched the others for a moment. Messy things. She peeled one bone away and nibbled at the scant meat along one edge. Delicious, but only about a half a bite. At this rate, she'd be eating until midnight. She wiped her hands and turned to her corn on the cob. That was something she'd eaten in the past. Another messy thing. Definitely not date-worthy. She gnawed a little and set it down before wiping her face and hands.

Her salad would have to do, and the fruit was delicious. She did attempt a few more bites of ribs before giving up on them.

"So Dani, what do you do?" Valerie leaned forward.

A hard question anyway, but especially at the dinner table. "I work for a crisis and trauma cleaning service." Details not necessary.

"Like a housekeeper? Oh, I bet you make a bundle." Lauren lifted one perfectly sculpted eyebrow. "I have a friend in Dallas who recently mentioned the trouble with finding a dependable cleaning service."

Jay started to say something, but Dani put a hand on his arm. Let them think what they wanted.

"Something like that."

"Wish I could get you to clean my house." Valerie leaned back in her chair.

"You do a fine job, Val. And you know a coach's salary isn't enough to have maid service." Buddy laughed. "But I bet you have insight on all of your clients don't you. Maids see everything."

"Oh, don't say that, Bud." Lauren put her manicured nails against her forehead. "Now, I'm gonna have nightmares about what mine has been finding in my trash can." She glanced back at Dani. "Hard work, but a noble profession. I'd never be able to do my job and keep my condo clean at the same time."

That conversation segued into Lauren's culture shock when she had moved into her condo in Chicago. And her job as a clinical psychologist specializing in behavioral issues and psychoses of teenagers. Very impressive, but that led to some exploits of the kids in town. That topic rounded into the crazy carryings-on that the home-town crowd had done when they were in high school together.

Dani watched her man. The way his mouth curled into a half-smile when he was embarrassed. She couldn't help but laugh when he got tickled during the stories. Some of them were funny, but most went right over her head.

As they began a friendly argument over something about their high school prom, Dani stood, picking up her dish and put Jay's on top of it so the others wouldn't notice what was still on her plate.

"You don't have to do that." Valerie jumped up.

"I like feeling useful."

Valerie followed Dani into the kitchen. "Just put them on the washboard there." She set down a stack as well.

"Where's your trash can?" At the very least she needed to discard her leftovers.

"Under here." She opened the cabinet under the sink. "But I have a strict rule about dinner dishes. Leave them for a later time."

Dani scraped Jay's plate and then her own into the trash. "I think I like your rules." Of course, she didn't mean it, but with the dishes in here, the mess wouldn't call to her to get busy and clean it up.

Buddy pushed through the doorway with some of the serving dishes. "What are y'all doing in here? Val, you want to have a little preview of Dani's work?" He guffawed.

"Don't be ridiculous." Valerie swatted at him with a towel. "I'm having trouble prying her away."

"Maybe I need to get Jay to toss her over his shoulder." Buddy winked.

Dani chuckled in response, but Jay had better not try it. "I'm coming. I'm coming." She gave a final look at the dishes, begging for a sink of soapy water. Maybe she should have been a maid.

Wait, if Buddy and Valerie were both with her, that meant Jay was in the dining room alone with the living mannequin. She sped through the swinging door.

"There you are." Jay stood and was, thankfully, all alone. "Thought you'd deserted me."

"No chance." She sat next to him. "Where's Lauren?" Not that she was overly anxious to discuss the woman, but she was distinctly absent.

"Had a call and stepped out on the front porch." He laced his fingers with hers. "Once she comes back in, you have to tell them what you really do."

She lifted her gaze to the ceiling. "It doesn't matter."

Buddy sat across from Jay. "What do you mean? You're not a maid?"

Dani gritted her teeth at Jay before smiling at her hosts. "I'm not that much more than a housekeeper."

"Who has solved murders." Jay leaned back in his chair, obviously enjoying his victory.

Buddy leaned forward as Val returned from the kitchen.

"Hunter-man, I thought you were the only cop at the table."

"You're a cop, Dani?" Val collected a large spoon from the sideboard.

"I'm not a detective." The last thing Dani wanted to do was talk about herself. "I clean up crime and trauma scenes."

"So you're a crime scene investigator?" Valerie carried a chocolate concoction and a small stack of bowls to the table. "Like Jay?"

"No, no. I only clean up after him." She smirked in Jay's direction. "And boy, is he messy."

Jay chuckled.

"Already cleaning up after him?" Valerie giggled. "The girls I know usually put that duty off until after the wedding." Her husband joined the joke.

Dani reddened. Stupid of her to set herself up like that.

"That reminds me. Joellen Daniels is getting married again." Valerie took in both Buddy and Jay with her glance.

"Isn't this three?" Buddy turned to Jay. "You

remember she married Henry right out of high school." He looked at Dani. "He was the quarterback."

"I remember." Jay pulled her hand with his up to the table and leaned forward.

Dani lingered over her dessert. A chocolate cake with a creamy topping, almost pudding-like, and cherry filling. Very rich. The others talked for almost another hour about memories and old friends. Lauren had drifted in at some point and jumped right back into the conversation.

Try as she might, she couldn't get over how natural Jay and Lauren were when talking together. Obviously they'd dated in high school. Had he been serious about her?

Marji Laine

Jay hadn't meant for the entire night to become a reunion of sorts. And it probably wouldn't have been if Lauren hadn't shown up. Every time the topic turned to current events, she'd diverted it back into ancient history with one story or another. Not that he hadn't enjoyed reminiscing, but he'd hated leaving Dani out of the conversation.

But his girl had been a champ all evening. And when they left, she'd even been nice to Lauren, giving her a hug. "It was so nice to meet you."

"You, too. Hope to see you again." Lauren had backed away from Dani and given Jay a much-too-tight squeeze. "Both of you."

He had peeled himself away and reached for Dani's hand as Lauren sashayed away.

Alone at last. He squeezed her hand. "Save me."

"There's a barracuda in the water?" Dani gave him a sidelong look.

"You okay?" He settled her into her seat.

"Sure."

He'd have to trust her answer because her face didn't seem all that enthusiastic. He climbed into his own seat, turned on the ignition, and shifted into gear.

"Sounded like you and the others had an amazing time growing up in Marseilles." Her voice sounded wistful.

"Borne from some crazy antics—thirty percent stupidity, twenty percent bravado, and fifty percent God's protection." He slowed at the four-way stop on the town square. "But you and I have good memories of our times together, too."

"Yes."

Was she upset with him? Lauren's greeting kicked at his conscience. Why did she have to do that? For the umpteenth time, he stuffed that regrettable issue down and tried to vary the topic. "Didn't you ever do anything silly in your past?" She had to have. Everyone did crazy, embarrassing things as they were growing up.

"Not really." She glanced out the side window.

The elephant had grown bigger than the truck cab. He had to talk through this with her. "Honey, if this is about that kiss… I didn't have time to even react."

"I hated seeing it." She kept her face turned away so that her voice was distant. "But I don't blame you for that. And I'm not upset, Jay. Not really. I simply realize the huge impact you've made on so many people. Why did you ever leave Marseilles?"

That was a tough one. Oh, he had an answer, but not one that he could share easily with his girlfriend. "It was time. I needed something new. Fresh. And Dallas held more opportunities for police work than Marseilles."

"You could have worked for your dad."

That had come up many times with his folks as well. "It's hard to explain."

"No. I think I get it. You needed to make it on your own. And you have. You are such a great man." She gave him a sad smile, almost like she was saying goodbye.

"You're biased." He pulled into his folks' drive much quicker than he'd expected. "And you were wonderful tonight." Stretching his arm toward her shoulders, he unlatched his seatbelt and leaned toward her.

"No. You... *you* are wonderful." With her enigmatic comment, she opened the door, jumped from the truck, and rushed up the steps to the house.

Her meaning dawned on him. She didn't think *she* was good enough? For *him*? "Dani, wait." Jay bolted from his side and dashed around the pickup bed, but the sound of the shutting door was the only response he got.

He lifted his face to the sky, popping his neck in several places. "I'm doing this all wrong, God. I don't know why this is so hard." Could the Lord be telling him that he shouldn't be continuing his relationship with Dani?

No. He didn't receive that. God had been blessing their relationship. Jay had even saved Dani's life. More than once. And he sure wasn't willing to let a few uncomfortable moments make him rethink his feelings for her.

He took a tour around the perimeter of his folks' property—such a haven. Had been a huge blessing for Mom and Dad, though likely still a strain on their bank account. He'd offered to help when they got the chance to buy it, but nothing doing. They'd done a remarkable job with it already.

He reached Mom's decimated garden. A white-faced, innocent-looking demon-cow stood near the gate chewing cud. Looked like she was laughing at him. "If it were up to me, you'd be burgers at the party on Monday."

She blew out a snot ball and turned her behind to him.

Continuing his tour, he prayed for wisdom with this relationship. So many things about Dani he adored, and yet her secrets continued to grate on him. How could he give his heart to a woman who couldn't be completely honest with him? But that was exactly what he'd done.

Again.

No. Not again. Dani wasn't Lauren. She wasn't the queen of hearts, the game player out for conquest. Dani was genuine and sincere about her affection and her emotions, even if she did keep things about her past under wraps.

Reaching the front of the house once again, he slipped inside the entrance. The master suite was dark. Not so strange. His parents had always been early birds. He took the stairs two at a time. Dark up here, as well. He'd hoped that maybe he'd find a glimmer of light underneath Dani's door. Something that might give him an excuse to talk to her again, but no such luck.

His dreams, that night, were full of futility and frustration. He awoke with a palpable foreboding that even his shower didn't wash away.

Thankfully, when he made it downstairs, his father and brother seemed to be getting along. Almost like normal.

Mom kissed his cheek. "Have a nice time last night?"

"Not bad. Though a little odd. Valerie had invited Lauren to join us."

"Lauren Stiles?" Her mom's face lit up. "She's such a sweetheart. I had no idea she was in town. But she visits her father often. About every other month or so. Of course, she's taking more responsibility with his recent stroke. Has full-time care that has to be arranged, and his banking and general care. Not to mention her full-time job in

Chicago. I don't know how she does it all."

"That musta been uncomfortable for your girlfriend." Dad eyed him over his cup of coffee.

"Was, I think, but Dani took it well." But then she never complained about anything. He took the glass of juice his mom had poured and tapped Kyle on the back of the head as he passed him. "How's the noggin?"

"Took him to the clinic on the freeway. Good catch on him getting those stitches." Mom poured a cup of batter onto the Belgian waffle press. "They don't think the scar will be much."

"Good to hear." Jay took a swig of the chilled freshness that brought him back to summer days in his mom's kitchen at the house in town. "Then you can keep your pretty face." He tickled his brother's ear, and Kyle swatted at his hand, laughing.

"Good to see you boys joking again." Mom tittered, and even Dad cracked a smile, glancing up from his phone. Used to be a newspaper at this time of the morning. "All we need is your sister, and it will be like old times."

"Kristi is *not* looking like she did as a kid." Kyle pooched his belly out.

"Won't be long now." Uncle Jay. Had a nice ring to it.

"She should be here in a few. She wants to meet your friend." Mom's grin faded.

Jay set down his glass. "I'm really sorry about your garden, Mom."

She waved it away like an irritating fly. "I don't want to think about it. And it wasn't Dani's fault as much as my own. But Tuesday morning I'll tackle the remains and the cleanup."

"You know Dani didn't do that on purpose." She had to believe that.

"Oh, of course. She just didn't know. So much a city-girl doesn't understand about the way we live." She poured herself a cup of coffee. "I don't blame her at all, for that. But that doesn't mean I think she's right for you, Jay."

"I really care about her." Sure, she wasn't

country, but neither was he. Not anymore.

"You hardly know her—"

"Caroline, we agreed about this." Dad's gaze shot up to Mom. She raked her glance across the ceiling.

"Agreed about what?" Jay cocked his head at his dad. So they'd been talking about Dani. They might as well tell him now rather than wait.

Dani peeked in through the door. "Oh, good. I was afraid I'd made a wrong turn."

Jay met her and pressed a kiss into her forehead. "How'd you sleep?"

"I don't know why, but I was totally conked out. I don't think I moved all night long."

"Country'll do that to you." Mom barely looked at her as she set the juice in the fridge. "Coffee's on the counter."

"Thanks, um… but that juice really looked delicious. Might I have a glass?"

Mom did an about-face and retrieved it. "Of course, dear. You're our guest."

Did Dani hear the formal pitch to his mom's voice? Hopefully not. She hadn't known her long enough to notice a difference like that.

The front door burst open, then slammed shut. Kristi bounced in, belly first. "There y'all are." She wrapped her arms around Jay's middle and dug her bony chin into his chest. "Big brother."

"Stop it, bully." He tousled her hair.

"About time you came back for a visit. Introduce me. I've been dying to meet your Dani." She stepped back.

"My sister, Kristi, and my nephew-to-be, Moofatta." Jay struck a formal pose.

Kristi shook hands with Dani. "That is not his name."

Dani chuckled.

"Well, you won't tell." Jay picked his glass back up. Served her right if the baby announcements had that name on them.

"In due time. Get it… due." She giggled.

"Ah-ha-ha. I get it. Pun-queen." He pushed a

plate of bacon toward her. "Have some breakfast."

"No way. I'm going shopping. Need a going-home outfit for the kid in here." She took Dani's arm. "And I wanna get to know your lady."

Dani laughed. "I can't imagine why you'd want me along. I've never even been around babies."

"Well, there are some darling shops downtown, and I could use a going home outfit, too." Kristi—the little engine that didn't take no for an answer—practically dragged Dani toward the front door, but by the time they reached it, his girl was fully immersed in laughter.

"Have fun." Jay waved at her. Kristi's spunk and enthusiasm were exactly what Dani need for a recharge.

Mom joined him at the kitchen entrance.

"I don't understand how you can judge her so brutally without even knowing her."

"Your mother is concerned." Dad came through the door and marched toward the master suite, but he slowed and turned. "That woman isn't like us."

Jay had thought Dad was warming up to Dani. "Weren't you just defending her?"

"I was merely trying to calm your mother before your friend arrived in the kitchen." So he didn't like her either. They weren't even giving her a chance.

"Why? Because she's never been fishing and doesn't know the different cuts of beef?"

"You know what I mean."

"Oh, come on, Dad. She left the gate open. That's a pain, but not a crime." The muscles in his neck tensed.

"That doesn't explain why she felt the need to eavesdrop on my personal conversation. Sneaking around corners and spying on us." His volume grew. "How long have you even known this girl, Jay? You know her parents? Her background?"

Wow, she'd really gotten on Dad's bad side. She did have curious streak, but that didn't make her a spy. "Her family is all gone. She's only been in Dallas about a year."

"And you know everything there is to know about her." Dad crossed his arms with his accusation.

Jay rubbed the back of his neck. Getting mad and defensive would solve nothing. Their attitudes had to have something to do with Kyle's wife. "Of course not. But I know her."

"She has no concept of boundaries." Dad paced a few steps away and the returned.

What could Jay say? He'd seen that trait in her before, but it had saved lives. "Sometimes that's not a bad thing. She's extremely observant. I told you about the crimes she's been able to solve."

"And put you in danger." Mom shook her finger.

"That goes with the job. You've been the wife of a sheriff for how many years?" It was probably different for a child than a spouse, but still. "And Dani didn't cause any of the problems. She actually helped solve them."

"Regardless of how you want to paint her tendencies." Dad patted Mom's shoulder. "She's put a terrible stress on your mother."

A low boil started at the back of his neck. They simply weren't letting their stiff-necked opinions go. He clamped his jaw tight for a moment, then responded. "I'm really sorry to hear that. I'll take her back home as soon as she and Kristi return." His shoulders stiffened. "Sorry I won't be here for your party."

Mom closed her eyes. "Jay, I'm sorry. I tried…." Mom reached up to pat his cheek.

"To what? Compare her to Angela? I'm not Kylc, Mom."

"I know." Again she looked at the ceiling. "I know. You're the eldest. Always responsible. I just get this terrible feeling…."

"It's called worry." Mom had always had an issue with it, especially when it came to her kids. "And there's no need."

"Are you sure you're not jumping at the first girl who comes along?" Mom lowered to the stool beside her.

Was she joking? "It's been a dozen years since Lauren and me."

"I don't mean her. I mean Kristi."

Dad put a hand on Mom's shoulder. "First your baby brother, then Kristi. Couldn't you be settling because you think you're getting past your prime?"

At thirty-two? Really? "No, Dad. I wasn't looking. In fact, I've had a couple of friends set me up with several ladies, but none of them interested me."

Mom nibbled on her thumbnail for a moment. "Look. Maybe you need a break from her to get your perspective. You'll be able to see if she's really as important to you as you believe right now."

Dad joined in. "Not a bad idea. You could return her to Dallas where she'll be most comfortable, then come home and let your mind clear. Speak to the Father about the two of you."

"You don't think I've already done that?" Jay walked to the staircase and turned back toward them. "Daily, Dad. I'm convinced the Lord has put us together. Clearly, neither of you share that conviction. I'm really sorry about that. I'm going to miss coming here."

"Don't be foolish, boy." Dad paced a few steps and returned. "You can't simply step away from your family. Not over some girl."

"She's not just some girl." His volume thundered. Didn't they get how important she was to him? "I love her. I want to marry her. I hoped to do that with your blessing. That you would embrace her as part of the family like you've done with Kristi's husband and even with Angela when Kyle insisted on marrying her."

"That was a mistake." Mom lifted her hands.

"Either way, you've made it plain you don't want Dani here." He'd never seen them be so judgmental and unkind.

"You watch how you speak to your mother." Dad pointed at him and almost growled.

"That's right, Dad. You defend the woman you love. That's what I'm doing, too. But let me be very clear. Whether we have your blessing or not, I will marry Dani. If she'll have me." He climbed the stairs and went into his room. What a disaster.

He pulled his suitcase from under his bed and laid it open on the comforter. Moving to the dresser, he cleared off several items, then stopped and stared in the mirror. He hadn't raised his voice to his parents since he'd begged them to let him play peewee football. And they'd been right. He was awful and got clobbered.

He turned and sat on the bed.

Please God, don't let them be right about Dani. About us. He mulled over their conversation for some time. Leaving sure wouldn't solve anything. With his suitcase only half full, he locked it up and shoved it under the bed.

What their dislike really boiled down to was

Dani's curious streak. They'd called her a spy. So what if she was a snoop at times. Why in the world would they care?

Unless they had something to hide.

Chapter Seven

Dani leaned against a counter while Kristi held scarves of different colors up to her face.

"I'm an autumn, so I'm told." Jay's sandy-haired sister posed in front of a mirror. With her light brown eyes, she could have been confused with her mom. "I'd say, with your creamy complexion, that you're a winter." She held a scarf under Dani's chin and pointed to the mirror. "See how well blues and purples light up your skin tone?"

And fuchsia. One of her favorites. "Mmm. I see." Though she hadn't been able to do a lot of shopping for anything besides jeans and tee shirts for some time. And she sure hadn't dabbled in her color palette.

Lauren Stiles shoved open the front door of the boutique and strolled in as if on a catwalk. "Here you are." Again in blue and white, this time her navy shorts and striped tank were set off with a thick coil of blue and white beads. Matching beads dangled from her earlobes.

"I was hoping to see you before you left town." Kristi squealed and went for a hug. "I heard about your dad's stroke. I'm so sorry."

"Thanks. I found a great home-care company." The blonde had to stoop to reach Kristi but squeezed her tight. "I've been in every shop on the square looking for you and called everyone in your family for your location. Don't you know a mother-to-be should always have her phone turned on?"

Kristi's jaw dropped. "Oh." She dug it out of her purse. "Oops. I forgot to turn the sound back up. Sorry about that."

Lauren gave a passing smile to Dani. "Good to see you again."

"Likewise." Dani mustered a smile in return. Too bad. She'd been enjoying every moment with Kristi, for the first time feeling like she could loosen up.

"How about lunch at the café?" Lauren laid a hand on Kristi's shoulder. "I've been dying for a turkey club on Storie's wheat berry bread. Can't get anything like that in Chicago."

"Or her father-in-law's spicy bread and butter pickles." Kristi gave the clerk several bills. "We've already eaten out on the highway, but I could go for a piece of lemon-icebox pie. So good on a hot day."

"I can't believe you didn't take Dani to the Storiebook Café for lunch." She looped her hand in Dani's elbow like they were besties. "You're going to love it. All the tourists go there."

"I'm up for that." Though sitting through another walk down memory lane with Jay's former girlfriend was far from her to-do list. After lunch, maybe she and Kristi could get another chance to talk. After all, Kristi had grown up with a lawman for a father same as Dani. In fact, they seemed to have quite a lot in common—well, except for Dani's foolish choices.

She held the door of the Texas Treasures Boutique open while Kristi and Lauren exited.

"I still think that violet number was perfect on you." Kristi swung her small shopping bag as she spoke. "Jay's eyes would have popped right outta his head."

It was pretty. Made her feel pretty, and she'd not felt like that since coming south. Not often, anyway. But that was part of the deal. She had to remove herself from everything she'd ever enjoyed. Friends, photography, a permanent church home, even shopping. Though in this tiny town, the shopping part wasn't such a big deal.

"Jay was always a sucker for pretty." Lauren came between her and Kristi, then turned away from Dani. "Did you hear how I made a fool of myself?" She regaled Kristi with the story of how she'd met Jay at dinner.

Dani tried not to relive the shock and embarrassment once more. Instead she examined the shops along the square. Jitters Coffee shop, Miss Dixie's Cottage, The Ice House. All historical landmarks according to the brass plates they displayed, but clean, cozy, and filled with delights for the eyes as well as amazing aromas.

"I know I must have seemed crazy." Lauren turned to Dani, stealing her attention away from the charm of the downtown.

"A bit of a shock." The image of her kissing Jay replayed in her head. Maybe she should get that violet dress.

"Well, put it out of your mind, my friend." Lauren put her hand on Dani's arm. "He clearly adores you."

Maybe the woman wasn't so bad. She focused on crossing the street as they bounded into a topic Lauren had brought up the night before. Something about hoodlums messing with her dad's car. The others turned left toward Storiebook Café, about a block away from the square and inhabiting what might have been an old gas station. Dani shot a look down a rather barren side street on the right. Not much there—boarded up buildings hugged one side across from an old convenience store. A woman hurried from behind the store and rushed across the street.

Wasn't that…. Dani stopped in the middle of the intersection. She turned and called to the others. "Isn't that your mom?"

"Where?" Kristi quick-stepped toward her.

Dani pointed, but the woman had disappeared. Shoot, she'd only glanced away for a second. The lady had to be around somewhere, maybe between the buildings? Dani moved in that direction.

"Are you sure it was her?" Kristi followed.

"I didn't see anyone." Lauren came alongside.

But Dani was sure. "Was your mom coming into town?" She hurried down the broken sidewalk to an alleyway and paused.

Kristi halted next to her. "She told me she couldn't get away. Said she had too many things to do for the party."

"Maybe she needed to pick up something." Lauren joined them.

Dani lifted her gaze skyward. "Like vegetables, since I single-handedly destroyed her garden."

Kristi giggled. "Oh, you weren't single-handed in that. You had at least a dozen hooves helping you."

Dani joined her laughter. This trip into town had been exactly what she'd needed. And Kristi was so much like her brother, except in the way of looks. "Well, there's no one here, now." Maybe she'd been wrong. "I can't imagine why she'd be visiting a closed store anyway." She pointed to the building directly across from her. *StopNShop* was displayed across a faded sign.

"You saw my mom come out of there?" Kristi

faced Dani. "No way. The folks wouldn't do business with Roger Basalind."

"Is that a clerk?" Lauren joined them.

"Owns the place." Kristi drifted closer to the store front. "You don't know him?"

The blonde shook her head. "Never heard of him, but I can think of better things to do than spy through the windows of a filthy, run-down rat's nest. Besides, it's closed."

Kristi checked the street, then stepped off the curb. "I've never seen this place closed. It was open yesterday."

Dani's curiosity sparked. "I'd think Saturday would be a big customer day." But it was certainly dark inside, and the neon *open* sign had been turned off. "Is it going out of business?"

"Hmm. Wouldn't be sorry about that." Kristi tried the front door. It wouldn't budge. "Sure might be, though."

"Who cares?" Lauren wandered toward the corner of the building. "Why don't I go get us a table?"

Something moved inside the store. Something large. And the movement uncovered the view of a foot sticking out from behind one of the store aisles. A shudder rippled across Dani's shoulders. She glanced at Kristi. In the bright sunlight, they were on easy display for anyone inside the shop. She tugged Kristi to the edge of the store, joining Lauren. "You both go over to the café you were talking about and wait for me."

"Sure thing." Lauren backed up. "This empty place has me a little creeped out."

She pulled on Kristi's shirt but released it when the bouncy brunette wouldn't follow.

"I'm not leaving you here alone." Kristi fisted her hips.

"There's someone inside. I think the store is being robbed. Call the police." Dani turned toward the backside of the building.

"You don't need to be here, Kristi." Lauren pulled on her again and stepped into the street that ran alongside the convenience store.

Kristi still didn't move but was already dialing. "What are you going to do?" Her eyes drilled Dani.

"See if I can find out what's going on." She darted down the side of the building and peeked around the corner. A door in back hung open, dangling on its hinges. She crept closer. Exposed nails stuck out from the broken facing as if the door had been forced.

Kristi joined her at the back of the building.

"I thought I sent you to the café." Dani's voice was barely a whisper.

"Lauren's more obedient." She matched Dani's volume. "But I'm calling the police."

Dani reached the open door. "I'm going in." She turned around and pointed at her. "Stay here."

Kristi tilted her head and gave her a look with furrowed brows that clearly argued against the wisdom of Dani's choice to go inside. It probably wasn't the wisest idea, but then Kristi hadn't seen what she had. There was someone on the floor in there. Someone who wasn't moving.

Dani crept inside and hugged the left wall, pausing to let her eyes adjust to the dimness.

A shadowy figure flew past her, crashed into the doorway, and let out a yell before disappearing around the corner.

Kristi screamed.

Shifting gears, Dani sprinted back into the sunshine to find Kristi on the ground. "Are you all right?"

"He ran off that way." She rolled to her side and pointed.

Dani knelt beside her. "Did he hurt you? Where did he hit you?"

"Not hit exactly. He ran past. I sort of lost my balance. I'm not even sure he touched me, now that I think about it."

Sirens sounded in the distance. "Are you sure you're all right?"

"I'm fine. Glad he came out before you went in there."

Dani glanced toward the opening. Had that runner been the person she'd seen? Surely not. A finger of smoke curled out the open doorway. "No, no, no!" She stood as the scent of the burn inside the building hit her nose. "Stay here."

Kristi clung to her leg. "You can't go in there. Something's on fire."

"Someone's inside."

With Kristi's release, Dani darted for the gaping maw. Sucking a lungful of clean air, she ducked inside and hurried toward the aisle she'd seen from the front window. Growing flames licked at the area. She stumbled across something and hit the floor, blowing out her held breath. She gasped and erupted into a coughing fit.

She edged forward. Sure enough, a man lay there, the flames engulfing the body. Definitely dead. She coughed again in the thickening smoke.

A ceiling tile fell. Too close. Recoiling, she bumped into a set of shelves. Cans rained down on her. Stunned, she squeezed her eyes shut several times to clear her vision. Her chest tightened. *God, get me out of here.*

Where had the exit gone? She faced where it should've been and moved that direction. A glimpse of light shown about ten yards ahead of her. Her knees raked across the gritty floor as fast as she could propel them. Her lungs craved fresh air, and her eyes burned.

With a crack, another lit-up set of tiles fell. Dani veered, losing sight of the doorway. Pieces of ignited ceiling tile cascaded around her. A piece of metal clanged to her left. Something burned her shoulder. Frantic, Dani pounded on her back and hair, praying the flame didn't catch her shirt. Smoke seared her throat. She coughed until bile rose to the back of her mouth.

A small explosion jarred her. Sparks showered the area, stinging her face and arms. She set to her course again, churning over residue from the ceiling. Some of it sharp, some still burning. Holding her final breath until her chest felt ready to burst, she made for what had to be the exit.

Smoke rushed out the open door, sucking into the outside like a twister. Her lungs seized. She gasped and choked, tripped on the door facing, and toppled forward. Her cheek took the brunt of the fall against the hot asphalt, but she couldn't even roll over to relieve the burn. Hands grabbed the back of her shirt. Her body shifted forward. A mask slipped over her face.

Someone picked her up and carried her farther into the bright sunlight. A fit of coughing seized her again as she squeezed her eyes shut against the day. Whoever carried her placed her on a cushioned bench of some sort, but when she started to sit up, he pushed her flat.

"You need to lie down a moment, miss." Deep voice.

She cracked open one eye in time to see the retreat of the firefighter heading toward the building.

A young man in a uniform took his place. "Lie

still please. Let the oxygen do its work."

Dani tried to comply, but Kristi's worried face came into her vision. "Are you all right? Oh, honey." She wiped at Dani's cheek, her eyes clouding. "I should never have let you go in that place."

Lauren appeared. "Oh, my gosh. You went in there? What were you thinking?"

The medic who had been treating Dani switched to Kristi. "Ma'am, I should check your pulse." He made her sit on the edge of Dani's cushion.

"Why?" Lauren came to her other side.

"Someone was in there." Dani could hardly make the words come out, but they were surely too soft for either Lauren or Kristi to hear them.

"Something's in your hair?" Lauren reached for Dani's head, but Dani shook it.

"Say again?" Kristi leaned close, watching her mouth.

"A body."

A wrinkle troubled her brow. "I don't understand."

Lauren touched her shoulder. "Somebody?"

The EMT's radio chirped. "Got a victim inside."

Dani pointed to the little microphone and nodded at the other two ladies.

"Oh, no." Kristi shut her eyes.

Lauren straightened. "You saw someone inside?" She leaned back down and peered into Dani's face. "Someone who's dead?"

Very dead.

Chapter Eight

"Dani went where?"

Jay's chest constricted. His sister's voice broke into tearful syllables over the phone line. He flung his fishing pole to the other side of a patch of weeds and raced up the path toward his truck.

Something about a burning building. And Dani. Dani inside. *God, take care of my lady*. He barely even saw the road that he flew down. Emergency lights flashed through the town square leading him to the back of the StopNShop. He stopped the truck, pulled it to the nearest curb, and shut it off. With his heart pounding a heavy bass through his skull, he made out the dark, curly head of his sister. He took off at a dead run in that direction, scanning the area as he went. Where was Dani?

God, please protect the baby and my sister, and let Dani be okay.

Lauren stepped in front of him with both hands up. "It's okay. Everyone's okay."

He scanned the heads of the milling people near where he'd seen Kristi. Firemen and police gathered at a darkened doorway. Gawkers filled in the areas between the cruisers and the fire engine. "Dani?"

"Is rather reckless." Her tone took on a superior note. "Going into a burning building? What… does she have a death wish?"

His scan stopped on Lauren's painted face. Words begged to be said, urged him to knock her down from her self-appointed pedestal. But that wouldn't find his girl. He laid his hands on her upper arms and peered into her eyes.

"Where. Is. She?"

She blew out a semi-snort and pointed to the ambulance. "She's fine."

"Thanks." He brushed past her and sprinted there. Kristi was sitting on the bumper arguing with a first responder trying to take her pulse. "Kristi, where's...."

His girl lay on a gurney just behind the EMT working with Kristi. Dani gazed up at him over an oxygen mask. "I'm all right." Her breaking voice didn't bear out her words.

He looked from Kristi to Dani as he breathed in the scorching smell. He'd rather have his girl's take on the situation, but Kristi could speak easier. He glanced at his sister. "Are you hurt?"

She shook her head. "Only my behind. I fell down when someone rushed out of the building. Had to be the guy who started the fire."

"What happened?" He glanced at Kristi, then peered at Dani. She had soot streaks on her face and blood on the front of her shirt. Her hands had been wrapped with gauze into white boxing gloves, and blue ice packs had been laid across both of her bandaged knees.

"Dani thought she saw Mom coming out of the StopNShop, but it seemed closed, which was odd."

"Dani's hands?"

"Small cuts and slight burns. They're wrapped with some ice packs." She shooed the EMT away when he tried to wrap a blood pressure cuff around her arm. "She has some burns on her arms. Musta seemed like Armageddon in there. And they're treating her for smoke inhalation, of course."

"Why was she inside? Who was the guy you saw coming out?" Surely Dani had a good reason for going into that place. Especially if it was on fire.

"She'd seen someone inside and wanted to, you know, look into the matter." Kristi shrugged.

When would Dani learn that she couldn't haphazardly investigate things just because she was curious? He knelt beside her and brushed a loose strand of hair off her forehead. "You could've gotten yourself killed, sweetheart. Why in the world would you do something so…" Lauren's words haunted him. "Reckless?"

Dani closed her eyes, and a soft tear squeezed out of one corner. Jay's heart melted all over again.

"Don't fuss at her, bro. I would have gone with her in a heartbeat if not for the little guy."

"Then I'd be chewing out both of you." He stroked Dani's arm. *Thank you, God, for protecting her.* He stared at the dark entrance again. What if she hadn't escaped? He'd not been here. Couldn't always have her back. With his jaw shut tight, he breathed out another prayer of gratitude and shoved the fear further down.

Windom Harris, chief of the Marseilles police department, pulled his cowboy hat off and wiped away a sheen of sweat on his smooth brown head. He stepped closer and waved his hand at Jay. "I don't want anyone talking until I get an officer over here."

Jay growled out an exhale, but he had no

jurisdiction here. He patted Dani's arm, straightened, and backed out of the chief's way.

Harris put one hand to his lips and let out a piercing whistle.

A young patrolman hurried over.

"Record all of this, Connors." The chief squatted near Dani's gurney, then looked at Kristi. "Mrs. Kincaid, since she's obviously unable to talk, I think I'll start with you."

Dani sat up and tugged at her mask.

"Whoa, there. You need that oxygen." Jay knelt again and tried to put the mask in place.

"I'll be okay for… a few questions." Her voice broke again, but the tone was strong.

"Very well." The chief knelt beside her. "I'll want to see your identification, but for now, how did you happen to be inside of the StopNShop during the fire?" He eyed the other officer who held his phone toward Dani.

"Wait, Chief Harris." Jay stepped between the other officer and Dani. "I don't like the idea of recording this conversation. Unless you're going to read her rights."

"Not arresting her for anything, yet." He looked up at Jay from over his rimless sunglasses. A challenge filled his voice. "Merely an efficient way of taking notes."

"Invasion of privacy." Jay folded his arms across his chest. "She doesn't relinquish her privacy to allow you to tape any conversation or answers to your questions."

"So now the big-city cop's an attorney. Is that it?" The chief stood with his hands propped on his waist.

Jay looked Connors. "Stop the recording, please."

The officer glanced at the chief, who nodded.

Harris smirked. "Feel better?"

"When it's gone." He glared at the phone, still in the outstretched hand of the junior officer.

The man cleared his throat and stuffed it in his back pocket before pulling out a notepad and a pen.

Jay stepped behind Dani's gurney once more.

"Don't be ridiculous, Jay. It's a simple question." Kristi pointed to a bag leaning against the wall of the building. "We were window shopping is all. Stopped at the boutique."

Harris called to a passing cop. "Retrieve that." He turned back to Kristi. "That doesn't tell me what she was doing at the StopNShop. Not exactly a window shopping type of place is it?"

"I'm right here." Dani lifted a wrapped paw.

Kristi didn't give her a moment to answer. "The shop was dark, and the front door was locked. Strange for a Saturday."

"Did she tell you that?" He pointed to Dani. What was he getting at?

"I tried the door myself." Kristi's eyes flashed.

The chief looked back at Dani. His gaze traveled from her to Jay and back to her. "That doesn't explain why you were inside, young lady. Especially if the front door was locked. Did you bust out the back door?"

"No." Dani's voice broke again.

Kristi chimed in. "Of course not, Chief. That would take a crowbar. Do you see a crowbar anywhere?" She held out her arms, her belly exaggerating the man's ludicrous statement.

"Mrs. Kincaid, I can't help but wonder why you see fit to answer all of the questions that I have for this woman?"

"I haven't suffered from smoke inhalation." Kristi lifted her chin. "And she's a friend of mine."

Jay cleared his throat. "Uh, actually, she's a friend of mine, Chief. Dani and I came to visit the folks this weekend. She and Kristi came into town to shop. Simple as that."

"Until she happens to get trapped in a burning building with a dead man." Harris lifted his eyebrows.

"What dead man?" Jay looked at Dani.

She nodded.

Had she gotten herself caught up in another crazy piece of intrigue?

"We didn't know anyone was dead." Kristi's voice had gone up a tone.

"I'd like to hear from her." Chief pointed at Dani. "What you were looking for in that place?"

Dani inhaled slowly. "I saw a foot sticking between the shelves..." Her voice, still crackled, was at least strong enough to hold a tone. "...when I looked in the front windows. I didn't say anything to Kristi because I didn't want to upset her, but then I saw someone moving around."

"So you thought it best to go in there?" The chief scrunched up his graying eyebrows. "Miss, do you have a habit of sticking your nose into places that might be dangerous?"

"Yes." Jay answered at the same moment that Dani did. At least she was aware of her risky tendency.

But the chief's flustered expression begged more details. Jay added, "Dani is a crime scene cleaner and has a curiosity that outweighs common sense sometimes."

Her eyes rounded. "Thanks." The word came out as a croak.

He was going to have to pay for that remark, but maybe his explanation would excuse her from any suspicion.

"Hmm." Harris looked down at her. "So you broke into the store to check on what you thought might have been a person lying on the floor in there. Was he dead?"

"I didn't *break* anything. The door was open wide. But with a fire starting, I couldn't leave someone in there. He was dead when I reached him, though. The body was part of the fire." Her voice strengthened as she spoke.

"How awful." Kristi's face crumbled, but no tears fell.

"Would someone get my sister some water?" Jay looked to the attendant still fighting with Dani to put the mask back on her face. The man dropped his battle and went to Kristi's aide.

"When I first went inside, someone rushed past

me."

"So there was someone in there?" The chief knelt again. "Can you describe him?"

"I wasn't even sure it was a him until he yelled. Sounded like a male voice." Dani swung her legs over the side of the gurney.

"He yelled?" The chief pulled out a pad of his own and jotted something with a pencil. Good thing. Judging from the chicken scratch of the other officer, the chief would need an expert in hieroglyphics to translate.

"He came barreling out and ricocheted off the broken edge of the facing where the nails are. He must have gotten a pretty good scratch if not a full-out puncture."

"Did you see this man?" He turned to Jay's sister.

"See him? He practically tackled me." She related how she'd fallen down when he'd rushed past.

Jay glanced at Dani's face behind the mask.

The Lord had blessed her again. Taken care of his sister and his nephew as well. Dani broke into a coughing fit. He knelt and stroked her back. Tiny holes were sprinkled across her tee shirt. "Lie back and let the EMT do his job."

She complied. Poor thing. She looked exhausted. But the chief continued the questions, more to Kristi than Dani, for another half hour before deciding he'd heard enough of the story.

The man laid his hand on Jay's shoulder. "I know she's your friend, Jay, but I need her to stay in town. You know the drill."

"Understood." Hopefully only for statements and not because she was a suspect.

The EMT unwrapped her hands and tossed the treatment bags into a cooler.

Both hands were reddened slightly but didn't seem too injured. He looked at the medic as the man loaded the chest into the back of the ambulance. "Is she all right?"

"Minor burns. Scrapes on her knees." He

removed those ice packs as well and climbed inside the treatment area. "I recommend more oxygen treatments at the hospital. Precautionary. You can take her yourself and save the transport fees."

She pulled down the mask. "No hospital." She sounded more like her normal self.

Jay didn't push it, but when he did get her and Kristi into his truck, he faced Dani. "This has got to stop."

"Jay, I only wanted to make sure—"

He held up his hand and shut his eyes. "I know you had a reason. You always justify your actions with pure logic, but you almost got yourself killed in there."

"It wasn't that bad, and—"

"And… this time, you endangered someone else." Jay wiped his hand across his forehead. "I know you, Dani. I know how bad you would've felt if something had happened to Kristi or the baby."

Her rosy lips thickened into a pout. "I'd never have been able to forgive myself."

"I'm a big girl, DJ." Kristi leaned forward, laying a fierce look on him. "I'm responsible for myself."

"This isn't about you, Kristi." He put a hand on Dani's knee. "Sweetheart, you have got to let the consequences of your actions enter your gray cells before you make a move." He pulled next to Kristi's car.

Without giving him a chance to assist her, his sister climbed down and slammed the passenger door shut before getting into her car.

Jay took the lead back to his parents' ranch. His girl kept her gaze diverted to the side window for most of the trip. "I'm not angry with you. Only worried."

"I know." She pulled her bandaged knees into the seat. "I was only focused on helping the person on the floor. I should have been thinking about Kristi, too."

"You should have been thinking about you." Jay let his exasperation raise his volume. "You were the one who could've been killed."

"There was someone on the ground. Smoke starting to seep from the building. What would you have done? Stood outside while someone, who might still be alive, perished in the fire that had only barely started?" She poked his bicep with her finger. "Don't pretend that you would've remained in safety, Jay Hunter. I know you too well to believe that. And to think that I should, simply because I'm a woman, is demeaning and insulting and ridiculous."

He probably deserved the rant, and likely it was only pent up emotions talking anyway. He stretched his arm over her shoulders. "Has nothing to do with you being a woman. It has to do with you being… well, *my* woman. He pulled into his spot at the end of the drive and sat for a moment, scanning Dani's smoky face. "I don't know what I'd do if something happened to you."

"Nothing happened. Not really." A gleam settled in her eye. "But someone did die in that building, Sherlock."

"Oh, no, Watson. Not this time. Neither the fire nor the person who died in that building has anything to do with us." Jay got out and rounded the nose of the truck. "Chief Harris is a good cop. He can figure this mystery out without any assistance from you."

"But if we could only…."

"No interest, no jurisdiction, no investigating. Got that?" He stroked the edge of her chin as Kristi drove in and parked behind them.

Mom came running down the steps to her car. "Are you all right? The baby?"

Dani stepped closer to him. "Oh, great. This is going to cement your mom's opinion of me."

"We're both fine." Kristi got out of her car and glared at Jay. "You weren't supposed to tell her."

He stroked Dani's back. "I didn't."

"Mrs. Phelps called and told me that you were in a fire." Mom wrapped her arm around Kristi's shoulders. "I would have come right away, but your dad was in contact with the office and got word that you were okay."

"Dani was in the fire, Momma." Kristi detached herself from Mom's hip and turned to look at them.

Mom turned and then gasped when her gaze landed on Dani. "I didn't realize." She rushed toward them. "Jay, you take her right upstairs. Kristi, get some ice packs for her knees." She did an about face and hurried up the steps. "I'll fix you some sweet tea, and we'll get you cleaned up."

Jay had to smile. He bent close to her ear. "See there. She doesn't hate you." What a relief. He'd been beginning to believe that his mom and dad had somehow turned into monsters.

"We'll see." Dani walked gingerly beside him.

He helped her into her room about the time Mom returned and shooed him away. Torn, he wandered out the front door. On the one hand, Mom was helping his girl. On the other, a twinge of worry about what Mom might say wandered across his shoulders.

His gaze dropped to where a bank of yellow daisies hugged the foundation of the ranch house. Looked like laughter on a stem. He tugged his pen knife from a front pocket. Mom might whip the tar out of him over this, but his girl deserved a little sunshine. He cut a fistful. Clutching them in one hand, he entered the house.

Mom stood in the living room fussing over Kristi. "I'm fine, Momma. And Dani didn't lure me anywhere. In fact, she tried to get me to go to the café with Lauren."

"Well, that's something." Sounded like Mom had started warming up to his girl. "I don't want her spying ways to rub off on you, though."

Or not.

"I'm not under high school peer pressure, Momma." Kristi's charm always won out when she called Mom that. If anyone could turn the woman's opinion of Dani around, it would be his sister.

He ascended the steps. Where was Dad during

all of this? Had he gone into town? And Kyle? Or did his brother have a job now? Jay should know the answer to that.

He knocked on Dani's door. "It's Jay."

"I think I'm going to turn in early. I'm a little sore."

Oh, no. What had mom said to her while he'd been cutting her a bouquet? "I brought you something. Would you just open the door for a second?"

She only opened it halfway and stood in the gap wrapped in one of his mom's robes. Her face was freshly washed, but her hair flopped over her head in a high ponytail and the smell of smoke still hovered. "How are your hands?"

"They're okay." She lifted them palm up. Little scratches but no real damage.

He revealed the flowers from behind his back and laid them in her hands, relishing the delight that sprung onto her face.

"Oh, Jay. These are so pretty." She glanced up

at him. "They look like the ones in the front flower beds." Her eyes widened and her smile fell off as her chin dropped. "No. You did not cut your mom's flowers."

He chuckled. "You needed them."

"But you're giving her another reason to be upset with me." She stepped within her room and tucked the stems into a tall water glass.

"Took them from the edge. She'll never notice." He stayed at the door but caught her slow movements. "You're not feeling dizzy or anything like that, are you?"

She shook her head and crept back toward him. "My knees. I can't imagine how babies can crawl all over the place. I went less than thirty feet, and I'm in agony."

"You want me to come get you for dinner?" The more his folks got to know her, be around her, the more they would like her.

"It will be hours before I succeed in chipping all of this gunk off of me. Besides, I don't think your parents are all that keen on spending extended time with me."

"They don't know you, yet."

"That's not the problem." She lowered her voice to a whisper. "I seem to have a knack for doing the worst possible thing around them. It's no wonder they don't like me."

"Honey, you're being too hard on yourself."

She shut her eyes for a moment. "No, really. I didn't mean to, but I did put your sister into danger. Just like you said."

He reached for her waist and pulled her closer. "I don't like you putting *you* in danger. Mom can't help being a mom. She'd worry over Kristi crossing the street at this point."

"I still feel terrible." Her eyes reddened.

He reached to kiss her, but she pushed him back, tears cascading down her cheeks. "Go away. I don't want you to see me like this." He stumbled backward, pausing as she pushed the door almost closed. "And thanks for the…" She took a ragged breath. "…flowers."

"Get to feeling better. I'll see you in the morning." Tomorrow would be a better day for Dani and his parents. After all, things couldn't get much worse.

Chapter Nine

Isolation isn't always a bad thing.

After Jay left, Dani sat in a chair next to the window and reached for her Bible. God's Word would sooth her, and did she ever need the comfort. Especially after Mrs. Hunter had made her view of Dani perfectly clear.

The conversation they'd had right before Jay brought her those cute flowers drifted back through her mind.

Mrs. Hunter had brought her sweet tea and some salve for her injuries. "I have to ask. What possessed you to go into that horrible place?" The woman's voice had been kind, but her eyes held something deeper. Something guarded.

Dani had explained, once again, about the man she'd spotted on the floor. She didn't mention thinking she'd seen Mrs. Hunter herself at the shop. While the woman applied the salve and re-bandaged the wide scrapes Dani had incurred on both knees, she'd showed no response at all.

Maybe if she'd revealed what had brought them to the StopNShop in the first place, Mrs. Hunter would have had displayed some reaction.

When Jay's mom had finished taping the gauze, she'd packed up her supplies. "I understand your need to help people, Dani. And I know that I'm almost a stranger...."

"You're Jay's mom, hardly a stranger."

With a sigh, Mrs. Hunter had continued, "I know that Jay has a dangerous job already. I've been a sheriff's wife for most of my life. But the thing is... Jay had never been shot before... well, before...."

"Before I came along." So much for soothing tension. "He saved my life, though."

"Exactly my point." The woman slumped. "Sweetie, I don't know how else to put it, but you've put Jay into unnecessary danger." She lowered her gaze to the floor. "I don't want to offend you, and I certainly don't want to upset my children, but now, you've also put Kristi into harm's way."

Kristi wouldn't have been in danger if she'd stayed at the corner of the building like Dani had told her. But that fact wasn't going to help anything.

The woman was right. Dani did stick Jay in precarious positions. He had been hurt more than once. And he'd even killed a perp who was about to shoot her.

He didn't like to talk about that much.

In the end, Dani admitted to Mrs. Hunter that she regretted all of the trouble she'd caused.

The woman had hugged her shoulders. "I know

you'll do the right thing, dear." Then she had left Dani to her troubled thoughts, made only more conflicted with Jay's visit.

Dani glanced again at the sweet flowers he had brought her. If only she could be a woman worthy of his affection. She leaned against the cushioned chair and looked out her window at the waning light. Even if Dani committed to staying out of trouble from now on, she was already in too deep. Her past permanently attached danger to her future.

How could she even consider bringing someone she cared about as much as Jay into that life?

Weird dreams left her with impressions of tragedy and dried tears in the corners of her eyes. She awoke, stiff but full of conviction, not long after dawn. Jay's mom was right—about her, and about their relationship. Dani was bad for Jay. Whether her dreams had confirmed it, or the reality had finally pierced her thick skull, he needed to stay away from her.

And she would make sure that happened. Today. An ache welled up inside her worse than any tooth irritation. She rolled over and shut off her alarm, biting off the pain that pulsed through her muscles. She must have aged thirty years overnight.

Struggling to sit upright, her gaze fell on the flowers Jay had given her the day before. Then bright and happy-looking, now they drooped around the edges of the water glass.

"Are you awake?" Jay knocked at her door.

"Just a minute." She shuffled to the door and pulled it halfway open.

"Sleep well?" His eyes held such compassion and devotion, she could hardly look at them. Instead, she examined his tie.

"Not really. I'm pretty sore."

"I was afraid of that." He took her hand. "The folks are leaving for church soon. I thought we should stay here."

"But you're dressed to go." And she couldn't bear to be alone with him. He'd change her mind again in no time. "I'm not myself. Please, go ahead without me?"

His dark eyes warmed with concern. "Your knees?"

That and other things. "I'd rather stay here where I can stretch them out without limping around in public like a little, old lady."

He tilted his head. "A beautiful, little, old lady." He sobered. "But I'm worried that you might have a serious injury."

"Nothing a little recuperative break won't solve." She coughed several times. "I'll get all of this out of my system."

"I'll bring you some pain meds. And how about some breakfast?"

He was so attentive. So kind. How could she purposely turn her back on this man? "No, really, I'll be fine. I don't want you to be late for church."

His brows furrowed. "You're my guest. I'm not about to leave you here alone when you're not feeling well."

"Please go. I don't want your parents to hold anything else against me."

"Aw, babe…." His mouth opened as though he was going to say more, probably argue the point, but he snapped it shut and paused for a moment. "At least let me bring you a tray? And a couple of ice packs?"

His kindness jeopardized her resolve. *God, help me follow through on this decision. It's best for us. Best for Jay.* "Hmm, I'm all right for now. You can leave me a plate downstairs if you have time. I'll come down later to eat, when I feel better."

He kissed her forehead. "I'd rather stay and help you. My folks would certainly understand."

"I've been a wedge between you and your parents since we arrived. And the truth is, I need to be alone for a little while." Was that terrible to say? "I need some time to work through all of my stiff muscles, so I don't walk around like a puppet."

Besides, giving Jay some personal time with

his mom and dad might heal the rift she'd sensed opening between them. This weekend had been hard on him as well.

Hopefully the decision she'd finally made would help all concerned.

Jay heaved a loud exhale. "If you insist." He lifted his dark eyebrows with his shrug.

"I do." She eased the door closed as he turned away. *I'm a monster.*

If only Jay had never taken interest in her. She certainly didn't deserve his admiration. Dani lowered herself onto the quilted comforter, sucking in the groan that begged to squeeze out. She stared through the crack in the floral curtains. Heat was already descending, drinking whatever moisture had been left from the cooler temperatures that the darkness offered. The day began like a pressure cooker, in more ways than one.

Jay was too good for her. Plain and simple. After all, she was criminal. A low-life. The very things that Jay hated and worked to defeat.

Her head had told her that over and over again, but she didn't want to listen. Now, she had to. Making this break was imperative, before the connection became so strong she couldn't cut through.

Her heart ached at the thought of running back to Dallas without him. Of not hearing his voice and seeing his smile every day. And not coaxing that cute dimple to show when he got tickled about something she said. *Ugh! This wavering back and forth. I know I need to leave him. Help me have the strength to follow through.*

After all, once he knew about her—*all* about her—their relationship would be over anyway. Better to pull the painful tooth now than to have it aching and stirring up frustration until the whole truth surfaced. And it would surface, by the trial if not before.

Her phone rang, vibrating on the dresser where she'd left it. Matthew.

"This is Dani."

"Glad you're still among the living."

She lifted one leg straight in front of her. Ow. "Don't be so melodramatic, Matthew." She bent over, stretching her muscle, then straightened. She silenced another groan and lifted her other leg.

"Another little piece of info for you before you judge me. A news story about your latest solved crime."

"The robberies?" Again, she bent over and stretched. The crime spree in Dallas had baffled her as well as the police. But she'd had the connection they needed to put all the details together. "Someone wrote a news story?" What was that reporter's name that she'd seen at the hospital?

He went on. "The article insinuates that you have special privileges with the police department. Says you were, 'found with several thousands of dollars of stolen money and valuables but somehow evaded what should have been an obvious cause for arrest.'"

"That's ridiculous. I didn't steal any money."

"Yeah, right." His tone barked of disbelief.

She straightened, her back popping. "I didn't." Wasted effort. To Matthew, she was nothing more than a little crooked pawn who was getting away with her crimes to catch a big kingpin.

"The story is complete with pictures."

Her chest convulsed. "Why didn't you mention that first?" For a witness protection agent, he had the flair of a thespian.

He ignored her. Per usual. "One of you, full face peeking out from behind that cop of yours."

Oh, no. "Does Jay's face show?"

"All three of you in vivid color."

Her roommate, too? "Tell me there aren't any names." How could she have let this happen?

"Not sure how they got them, but yours, his, Tasha's are all included in the caption. Tonio is part of the story, too."

Jay was named? Pictured? No. Now he and Tasha were stuck in the soup with her. "Is Tasha—"

"I've got a bodyguard watching her. She's fine, though we're going to have to make some adjustments to our plan. Probably move her for the duration."

No. She was so close to getting her law degree.

He barely took a breath. "And we've got to get you back to Sacramento."

"Wouldn't that be the first place Robert would look?" She stood, her knees screaming. "What about Jay and Tasha? They don't even know the danger that they're in. If the story is as you say, all the links are in place to find me." As gently as she could, she knelt. The burning of her muscles and the ripping of her raw skin put tears in her eyes. She reached under the bed and pulled out her suitcase.

"Why do you think I'm calling? I know you're brilliant and all, but I'm pretty good at my job without your help, and I have the record to prove it. Until you…."

"Right, until I came along. I know. I take more of your time and effort than all of your other clients."

"Combined, but who's keeping record." He actually chuckled. She'd never heard him give the slightest indication of a personality. "Seriously, things are going to get tougher from here on in. I know I've been giving you grief these past few months. It's part of the training to help you learn independence all over again. But you kept throwing wrenches into the works by getting yourself into dangerous situations."

"So your fussing has all been an act?"

He cleared his throat. "Not all of it. Most. But now, we've got some real work to do. You have to commit to doing exactly as I say. Both of our lives will depend upon it. Can you do that?"

"What about Jay? And Tasha?"

"I've got an idea on how to take care of them. But you're going to have to come clean and cut ties." His words sliced through her heart.

But that's what she'd decided anyway. Why should him insisting on the same thing upset her so?

If nothing else, the Lord was showing what He wanted even clearer.

She released a ragged breath. "I'm packing now. I'll call a cab to take me to the bus station." Using the case and the bed as crutches, she pushed to standing. Her back ached even more.

"Bus? No. You stay in Marseilles until I can get an agent on you. I'll give you a call when we have one in your area." His voice had an edge of concern.

"You really are worried."

"The path is too well-lit. If Robert hasn't heard what happened to Tonio by now, he will. And soon. Despite the alterations, he can't help but recognize you." He cleared his throat. "I'll feel better when I've got you under my own surveillance and out of Dallas."

Maybe Matthew did care, a little.

Jay dished out a plate of biscuits and eggs and

left it on the warming zone of his mom's stove. He put another plate on top of it to keep the biscuits moist. Hopefully Dani would see it.

He couldn't blame her for wishing to remain at the ranch. Not with all she'd been through.

"How is Dani feeling?" Mom put a hand on his arm.

"In her words, not herself." He pursed his lips together. "She looks miserable, and I feel helpless."

"I don't wonder that she's terribly sore after yesterday." Dad stepped into the kitchen and picked up a mug. He filled it from the steaming coffee pot on the burner.

Jay took a sip of his coffee.

"I really don't wish to talk about all of that again." Mom's eyebrows wrinkled together. "I know she's your friend, Jay—"

"She's more than a friend."

"Exactly. Her curious nature has brought you both trouble in the past, and this time, your sister was almost hurt."

Jay ground his teeth. "Kristi's a grown woman, and she has more than a little curiosity herself. After all, she grew up in the sheriff's house."

Dad paused, his cup halfway to his mouth, and pierced Jay with a dark glance. The same one he'd used on suspects when Jay had done ride-alongs. "Kristi's lack of judgment isn't my current concern. Seems plain to me that this girl, regardless of her reasoning or suspicions, looks for trouble."

Had Dad spent more than twenty minutes with her? "You don't even know her. How could you already make up your mind?"

"I've seen enough. I'm sure she's delightful, but she's also nosy and unwise in her actions." He sipped his coffee and set it on the counter. "I'm only trying to save you from the pain that Kyle dealt with when he didn't listen to our counsel."

"I'm not Kyle. But if I remember correctly, you gave his girlfriend several months before you made a decision about her."

"By then, they were engaged. We don't want

you to follow his path." Dad's gaze lowered to the tile floor. It was settled.

"You're not even willing to have lunch with her?" This wasn't like Dad, cemented into his decision simply for the sake of the concrete. "I remember, as sheriff, you always kept an open mind, even when evidence seemed to make guilt obvious, until the jury convicted."

"She's not a criminal. She's building a strong influence over you, son. I want to protect you from someone who has shown herself to be foolish." Dad lifted his chin.

"We only want to keep…." Mom hesitated and shifted her eyes toward Dad. "Family is most important."

Unbelievable. "Fine. You've made your decision, though it has no rationale. I'll have to make mine, without regard to your opinions." Obviously, his decision yesterday to leave had been the correct one, even if he hadn't been able to take that action.

Dad let out something of a growl and set his mug hard on the counter. "Out in the car. We will speak more." He gave Jay a fierce look and went the back way toward the master suite.

"Don't be too hard on him, son." Mom patted his hand, then pulled her key chain from the hook beside the door. "You know your father never does anything without good reason." Her face seemed to crumble as she opened the door. Was she crying?

"Mom."

She didn't give him a chance to speak further but closed the door after herself. What was going on?

No longer interested in eating, Jay made his way to the entry hall where he'd left his Bible. He sauntered out, trudging down the steps from the front porch, and followed the cobblestone path toward the drive. Kyle's truck, windows down again, took up one side of the parking area. Hopefully he didn't leave them open like that during the other three seasons of the year. Jay opened the door to roll one up and found a metal coffee mug in the cup holder. One of the more expensive designs. Deserved better care, like maybe washing? But he lifted it to check for more of what he'd found before.

Clear underneath this time. Good. Just to be sure, he opened the glove box and gave that compartment a quick look. Ancient owner's manual, some breath mints, a tire gauge. Nothing that hinted of drug use.

Kyle had been a good kid. Despite whatever was going on, seemed he still was, at least in this area.

Dad pulled the car even with him and honked. Jay tucked Kyle's coffee mug back into the holder and rolled up the driver's window. Reclaiming his Bible, he withdrew from the car and shut the door.

Before Jay could even get settled in the back seat of the sedan, Dad started in on whatever was eating at him. "How much do you know about Roger Basalind?"

Jay let the name rumble through his mind a few times. "I don't think I've heard of him."

"Didn't you go to the StopNShop for the chips the other day?" Mom turned in her seat to look at him.

"Yeah. The guy there was Dawson Keist. I went to school with him."

"Works for Basalind." His dad glanced at him through the centered mirror.

Basalind must've been the bullet-shaped guy. "I guess he's the one who came in while I was there." Time to dig into the center of this issue. "Told me to tell you that he'd only do business with Mom from now on." He let that sink in. "Considering that the place has become sort of a way station for the drug movement in the area, what business could y'all possibly have with the man?" Not that they could be involved at all with drugs. But if Kyle wasn't, then what was going on?

Dad's eyes didn't move for a moment.

Mom's finger went to her lips, curled over

them as if to keep them shut. She finally moved them. "This has nothing—"

"Caroline." Dad reached across the gap in the seats and put his hand on her knee. "I'll do this." He replaced his hand on the wheel. At ten and two like always. "I put myself in a… position that was inappropriate… for a sheriff. And wrong on a personal level, for all of you."

Inappropriate? All sorts of alarms began to clang through Jay's head. He pulled in a deep breath. So many things fell under that category. Jay didn't even want to begin to visit them all.

"Gambling."

Mom pulled a tissue from the box wedged into the console and sniffed.

Jay gasped and blew out his lungful. *Inappropriate* could have been so much worse. "I never knew you—"

"Let me get this all out." His dad lifted a hand. "I went overboard at one point. Extended myself beyond… I owed the gambler… well, quite a sum.

Took over a year to pay it all, but we were able to."

Repaid the guy *and* kept the ranch. Something wasn't right about that.

"Trouble was, we'd only just purchased the ranch. I had to get a little help to repay the casino owner."

"Oh, Dad, you didn't." Pieces came together.

His father glanced up into the mirror. "Basalind gave me a long-term loan so I could pay off the debt."

"That's why you had to step down from running for sheriff. You couldn't be connected to someone who might be associated with drug running." How could his dad make such a foolish mistake?

"I was unaware of that at the time, but yes. I couldn't allow anyone of questionable character to have such influence over me." A wrinkle formed above Dad's brow. "I didn't realize, at the time, that he'd made an alliance with Art Fowler."

Jay had a vague impression of a tall, gangly

man with a rounded chin and a permanent scowl. "How do I know him?"

"His son was your brother's best friend back in high school. For a while."

Oh, *that* Art Fowler. No wonder Dad practically spat his name. "Is Fowler the new sheriff?"

His dad nodded. "Basalind's… enterprises have flourished since then." Dad's eyes, shown in the mirror, hardened as his eyebrows drew together.

"But the StopNShop is in city limits." Surely, Basalind didn't have that much power.

"Chief Harris is a good man, a good cop. But he always allowed me, as sheriff, to take the lead. Unfortunately, seems he's doing that with Art Fowler, too."

At least Jay knew what was bugging his folks so much. "I've saved up a little money. Can't I see about paying Basalind off?" The county would re-elect Dad in a moment given the chance.

"Not your problem, Jay. Besides, if I run again,

I'm putting a target on the rest of the family. Fowler's already been trying to concoct some reason to throw Kyle into jail."

"But Old-Man Fowler didn't beat him up. Right, Mom?"

"Looked like Basalind's car. Old, black SUV, but it was too far away to be positive. I wouldn't have known my own son so far away had it not been for his truck." She sniffed.

"Deputy even stopped Kyle on his way home from the clinic last night." Dad scowled.

"Let me guess—broken tail light?" Probably why they had been broken during the fight.

His dad continued. "That was the excuse, but the deputy had him lying on the ground in front of his truck while he did a full search, but he had to let him go."

Whoa. Wait a minute. "I found a packet of cocaine in the truck yesterday afternoon, after that fight y'all saw." Now, the drugs made sense. Obviously, one of the *fighters* had planted the packet while the others kept his brother occupied. "Dad, you need to talk to a Ranger friend of mine about this."

"Not now, I won't." He turned right into the lot of Pinehaven Church. "And if you love us, you'll keep this all to yourself."

"Did Dani hear you fighting with Basalind, then? Or was it with the sheriff?"

"Basalind wanted an extra percentage for the loan. Threatened to make things easier for Fowler to trap Kyle if I didn't comply."

Jay weighed Dad's information. "Maybe you should send Kyle out of the county for a while. Until you can pay off Basalind or until Fowler is beaten in his election.

"Basalind's no longer an issue. He was the victim in the StopNShop according to the word I got from Chief Harris."

But that meant Kyle could be a suspect. He had a darn good motive for killing the man. And so did Dad.

Marji Laine

Chapter Ten

Dani watched Jay and his parents drive away. A minute later, Kyle banged down the stairs, and his truck roared off as well. Silence settled over the house. Well, besides the constant chatter of songbirds outside her window.

She showered, letting the hot water ease away the soreness in her shoulders and back. She gingerly dressed and packed, all the while practicing the speech she would need to persuade Jay let her leave.

If only Matthew had given her permission to escape while they were all at church.

Still, he promised to help her leave. That would give Jay's family time to heal. His parents would be able to welcome their first grandchild with no other concerns. And Kristi's focus right now should be all about bringing her new child into the world instead of keeping the peace between Jay and her parents.

Besides, the last thing she wanted to do was find out the Hunters truly had something to hide. That would crush Jay. Her too, especially if she had to be the one to tell him.

Straightening the room to the way it had been when she moved in, she contemplated Matthew's possible plan. No matter where he sent her, the move would be complicated, but returning to Sacramento? How could that be a good thing?

She lugged her suitcase down the steps and stashed it in the coat closet. Wouldn't do for any of them to find it before she was ready to leave.

Her whole body ached at that point. An enchanting aroma drew her into the kitchen. Mrs.

Hunter's wonderful biscuits and a small bowl of sausage gravy sat on a warmer. Yum.

Jay's mom was an amazing cook. Yet another good thing about Dani walking away. Her meager skills in the kitchen would never satisfy Jay. And she'd hate to doom the poor guy to a lifetime of dry pot roast or frozen dinners.

She touched the frame of his senior photo, displayed with those of his siblings' over the kitchen table.

God, give this man the perfect wife. Someone who will match his intellect, challenge and encourage him. You did such an amazing job with him, and he loves You so. Please bless him with a woman deserving of him, and one who sparks the affection of his family, too. They mean so much to him.

A tear dropped to her cheek. She was not that woman.

She glanced at the clock and wiped the tear away. The family would be returning anytime, and crying wasn't an acceptable way to past the minutes. Instead, she collected the plate left for her and enjoyed a final meal in this beautiful house.

A knock at the front door caught her by surprise. No one in the family would knock. She left her seat to peek around the corner across the entry hall. The lead cut-glass in the front door revealed someone standing there. Cowboy hat. The figure leaned closer and knocked on the glass again.

If someone was knocking, they weren't up to trouble. Could this already be the agent Matthew had sent? She crossed the wide foyer, unlocked the deadbolt, and pulled the door open.

A uniformed county cop with graying sideburns stepped inside. His wide smile didn't reach his striking blue eyes, but he slipped off his hat and bent to address her as though she were a child. "Sheriff Fowler, ma'am. I don't suppose any of the family is here?"

"If you didn't expect to find anyone at home, then why are you here?" Dani stepped back another pace and crossed her arms.

The man chuckled and straightened. "I'd heard you were pretty but didn't realize you were quite that smart." He turned and pushed the door closed. "Fact is, I need to speak to you and have been waiting to have our conversation… in a more private setting."

"And you knew I was here because…?"

"I've had a deputy keeping an eye on the place. At least until I could have a chance to talk to you." He moved farther into the foyer.

She circled him. "So your office has kept an eye on the place?" The back of her neck tensed. Something was very wrong about this set up. She pushed past the sheriff, opened the front door, and stepped outside. "You'll have to talk out here, then, where there are people watching." She turned around and eyed him through the opening. "For one thing, you don't have a warrant or permission from the home owner to be inside. And for another, I don't entertain strange men, even professional ones, when I'm alone."

He poked his hat back on his head and stepped onto the front porch. "Fine with me."

She closed the door behind him. "What do you want, Sheriff Fowler?" Bracing herself for his answer, she took in every movement he made, from the way his hands couldn't find a comfortable position to his eyes drifting toward the garage on his right. Maybe that was where his man hid and observed.

"I believe you left something out of your discussion yesterday with Chief Harris."

"I can't imagine what you mean."

"The fight you observed? Seems Kyle Hunter had a messed-up face when he got to church this morning." He shifted his weight to one side. "Word is that Roger Basalind was one of his exterior decorators, so to speak."

Dani resisted reacting to his question, but volts of electricity bounced around her insides. He wanted to implicate Kyle. But how had he known that she'd witnessed the fight? "Interesting. I don't actually have any information for you."

"You telling me you didn't witness any fight?"

"I saw someone hit someone else." She nodded. "I haven't actually met Kyle or the other man you mentioned, so I couldn't possibly say either of them were involved. I can't even say it was a fight since I saw nothing but the first punch."

"You witness a punch-out and then calmly go about your business?" His frazzled gray brows drew together.

"No, we went to see if we could help." Shoot. He'd drawn her right in. She clamped her teeth together and awaited his pounce.

"We? I thought your boyfriend was in town and all that…."

"How is it you know so much, Sheriff? You do realize that recording devices are illegal, invasion and privacy and all that." She glared at him with her eyebrow raised.

The man raised his hands in mock innocence.

"This county has no need of more bugs." His chuckle had a false ring to it. "The gossip mill is quite up to the task of keeping me informed about most everything that goes on."

Probably true, but he had a guilty tilt to his head. "So we're finished here? I have things to do."

"So who else was with you, and how did you get out to the road?" He put his hands on his waist. "You did go out there, right? To see if someone needed help?"

"I think I'm through with answering questions." He already had circumstantial guesswork going against Kyle. No way was she going to add Mrs. Hunter to that stew pot.

"Maybe I should explain that several people saw Caroline Hunter leaving the StopNShop moments before your little group went over there." He let his gaze drop to the toes of his boots, and he leaned back against one of the supports for the porch roof. "She took you out to the site of the fight, didn't she?"

Football time. Dad had been a huge fan and compared the game to his detective work all the time as she grew up. In this case, she had to change the ball possession. "What could the fight possibly have to do with the fire?"

"Simple. Man number one beats up man number two. So man number two kills man number one. Or, as I believe happened in this case, someone from the family defended him."

"And Mr. Basalind was man number one or man number two?" She folded her arms over her chest.

The sheriff's gaze drifted to his left. "Man number one."

"So he was the one getting beat up." Dad's ball possession gag always worked great.

"No. He was the second man, then." His ruffled brows furrowed even deeper.

"Oh, so he wasn't the man doing the fighting." She had to work not to giggle.

"No, he was."

"Aren't you sure? You said he wasn't, then he was. Are you even sure he's dead?"

"Yes. I know he's dead." His irritation grew in proportion to his confusion. "Kyle Hunter...."

"Beat him up?" She lifted innocent eyes toward the man. "Then why would he go to the effort of killing him? He'd already gotten the upper hand and walked away."

Fowler's gaze fell as his eyes turned fierce with concentration. "He... wait."

With a rumble and a tiny cloud of dust, Mrs. Hunter's silver sedan cut through the tall pines as it followed the curve up to the garage. Not a moment too soon. "Maybe it would be better if you asked them."

Sheriff Fowler watched the car and turned a furious face toward Dani, then he seemed to paint on a pleasant demeanor. He even laughed as he reached out and touched her shoulder. "I'm gonna do that very thing, young lady. Thank you for thinking about stepping outside to the porch. I'll let them know we've been having a nice, little chat."

With plenty of innuendo that Dani had implicated them in this murder, no doubt. She went cold. This man wasn't all that quick-witted, but he was scheming. Well, if he wanted to play games.... She rushed into the house and pulled her suitcase out of the closet and onto the porch as Jay and his folks rounded the edge of the house. "Could you ask me all of your questions on the way to the bus depot?" She pushed the bag's handle into the sheriff's hand and widened her eyes. "It's a shame you didn't get here before the family came back." There, that should take care of his intentions to drag her into his fantasies.

Jay climbed the steps and took one of her hands. "You're leaving?"

Dani could scarcely look upon Jay's disappointment. "You know it's best." Her game-face slipped. This part was no facade. She couldn't possibly stay another day making Jay's parents so miserable. "I'm ready to leave if you are, Sheriff."

She turned to the surprised man.

His face settled into an ominous tone. "You know I didn't come here to cart you to the bus station."

She tilted her chin? "I thought you wanted to ask me questions on the way?"

He glanced from her face to the others as Kyle's truck rattled up the drive. At least she'd get to meet him before she left.

"Why did you come here, Fowler?" Mr. Hunter was a half-foot shorter than the man but strode forward with the presence of a lion. "You certainly knew that we would not be home."

"I have witnesses that place your wife at the StopNShop before the time of the murder." He released her suitcase, then descended the steps toward the others.

"And you came to try to cement that vague statement with something twisted from our house guest?" Mr. Hunter spit into the yard. "That's low even for you."

Sheriff Fowler pointed in her direction. "The girl said she clearly saw the fight."

"I clearly saw nothing." Well, nothing *clearly*.

"Saw your son getting beat up." He kept his finger toward her.

"I don't even know their son." Dani kept her expression wide open.

"And your wife was standing right next to her."

"She was…." Dani halted. She'd become so good at lying, yet everyone would peg her as dishonest if she let the falsehood fly again. "What? I never told you anything like that."

Slightly late, but almost on cue, a battered young man who must've been Kyle Hunter sauntered across the lawn. He didn't even look at the sheriff but ascended the steps. Shifting his Bible, he extended his right hand. "You must be my brother's girlfriend. About time we finally met."

Dani shook with him and smiled. "Dani Foster."

"Kyle Hunter." He winked at Jay. "Good

choice, bro. Mom, is lunch on? I'm starved."

Fowler cleared his throat. "And as for you."

Kyle slid his gaze to the sheriff. "Oh, you're here." His smile turned into a snarl. "How nice."

"You might want to ignore, me, hoodlum…." Fowler marched across the lawn to the drive.

Jay glanced down at Dani. "What is going on?"

"From what I can tell, your sheriff is trying to pin the murder on your mom. He tried to trap me into implicating her. But I don't know what he's doing now."

"You have an open container in here, Kyle Hunter." The sheriff's shout sounded downright jubilant.

Open container? Not good. Not good.

Jay leaped from the porch and sprinted across the yard as Fowler opened Kyle's truck door.

Slipping his phone from his pocket, Jay took a stance to view his actions through the open passenger window. "I'm recording an illegal search, Sheriff."

"You put that camera phone down. I have an open container and am within my full rights to investigate."

"No one is driving this truck. You didn't stop it. And it has been completely out of your view for at least a full minute." He stepped closer. Yep. The same metal coffee cup sat in the holder. "Plenty of time for anyone to set a simple cup in a holder."

"Don't be ridiculous." Fowler reached for the cup.

Jay extended the phone in front of him to get a good angle. "Touch anything inside that car, Sheriff, and my family will be suing you for unlawful entry, illegal search, police harassment, trespass, and I might even press charges for breaking and entering." His dad and mom came alongside him.

The man paused and looked into Jay's eyes. *That's it. Recognize that I mean every word.* He kept his eyes steady on the man's face.

Finally, Fowler withdrew his hand and closed the door. "I'll be back with a warrant."

Fat chance. Though the man was certainly bent on ruining their family. Jay put his phone back into his pocket. Either way, he'd share this video with his Texas Ranger friend and see what avenues might be alternatives to investigate the way Fowler ran the county.

Kyle rounded the front of his truck. "I don't know why, Sheriff. I don't have anything in there worth finding." He leaned against the truck and winced as his shoulder hit the frame. Pulling away from it, he straightened, but pain poured from his eyes.

Fowler lifted his chin. "What's the matter with you, boy?" He'd noticed the look as well.

"Nothing. Just a hot roof." Kyle backed away a little.

Laying his hand on the roof, Fowler tilted his head. "Not really. Cooler today than the last few."

He stepped closer. "Something wrong with your shoulder?"

Kyle retreated another pace. "No. Sore muscles are normal. You know." His face reddened.

Jay glanced back toward the house where Dani stood. She looked back at him and shrugged. At least, this time, she'd stayed well away from the trouble.

Lightning fast, Fowler darted for Kyle and grabbed his upper left arm. His brother let out a yell and went down on one knee.

"What are you doing?" Jay rushed forward.

"Take your hands off of my son." Dad's voice boomed over the shock and motion like a cannon, but Sheriff Fowler had drawn his weapon and pointed it at Dad.

Jay halted but put his palm against his father's chest. "There's no need for that."

"I say there is. I'm arresting a suspected murderer, and his family is attacking."

"No one is attacking you, Arthur." Dad retreated a few feet, dragging Jay by the forearm. "But there is no reason to arrest Kyle. This is ludicrous."

Fowler smirked. "Something your girl there told Chief Harris." He looked up and his smirk faded.

Jay followed his glance. Dani stood at the near railing of the porch with her camera phone firmly in her grip. "Go ahead, Sheriff Fowler. You're live on Facebook. Should go viral."

"Put that phone down." The man growled and shifted his aim in Dani's direction.

Jay moved sideways. "It's only a camera." He lifted his hands, though he could hardly shield Dani in her elevated position.

"Are you going to shoot me on a live Facebook feed?" Dani's voice betrayed her fear. She wasn't challenging him with sarcasm. Her question was one of genuine concern.

The sheriff squinted up at her, then holstered

his weapon. "Well, since this is a live feed. I've just caught a murderer." He pointed to Jay. "Your friend reported that the man who fled the scene banged his shoulder against some bare nails on the door facing. I'm betting that your brother there has some pretty deep gashes." He turned to Kyle. "Hope you've had a recent Tetanus shot." Fowler leaned over and started reciting Kyle's rights to him as he pulled him to his feet.

Jay kept his distance, lest the Sheriff go Dirty Harry on them again. "Kyle, tell him it isn't true."

His brother's head went down, but he grimaced as the sheriff clicked hand-cuffs into place. "I'm going to need a lawyer." Kyle ducked his head as the sheriff shoved him into the back of the squad car, but he looked back at his brother. "I didn't kill Basalind, Jay. I could never kill anyone."

The sheriff slammed his door closed and scowled at them before getting in his cruiser.

"Dad, can't you do something?" Jay watched the SUV roll out of sight around the bend.

His dad muttered something, then he turned away and hiked to the porch. He passed Dani without so much as a glance.

Mom followed him but paused when she reached Dani. "Do you feel better?" Her voice seemed tense, but her face showed genuine concern.

"Yes, ma'am." Dani held his mom's gaze but didn't smile. "But I still need to go."

Jay took the porch steps two at a time. "She's not leaving, yet." He grabbed the handle of her suitcase and wheeled it back inside. She was staying. They both were. At least a little longer. Even if he had to hold her suitcase hostage to make it happen. He hauled it up the stairs to the second floor landing.

"Jay, you bring that right back down here." Dani paused at the door, then ran up the steps behind him. "Stop being childish."

He reached the top and shoved the case through her open doorway. "Childish is running away just because things become a little tense."

"A little…." She lowered her voice to a whisper. "My evidence has sent your brother to jail. There's no way your parents will let me stay here, let alone continue to be your girlfriend."

"Uh-uh." He sliced the air with his hand. "They have no say in that. It's your choice and mine."

"Maybe I've been choosing wrong." Her gaze climbed to his eyes.

Jay let a moment of silence pass. "You really mean that?"

She hesitated, then lowered to sit on the top step, her chin in her hands. "I don't know what I mean."

Jay nudged her to the right and squeezed in beside her.

"I do care about you, Jay. You know that."

He put his arm around her and stroked her back. "Is there a *but* to that?"

"No. I'm in…." She took a breath, almost like

a gasp. "Uh… worried. How can there be any future for us if your family dislikes me so?"

Million-dollar question. At least he had learned the source of their strain. "Honey, this isn't like my parents. At all. I can't explain everything, but their problems don't have anything to do with you. And once the tension from the real trouble eases, you'll see who they really are. Caring, funny, and light-hearted." Even as he said it, the words usually describing Mom and Dad seemed implausible.

He took one of her hands. "If you still want to leave, I'll take you home right now, but you have to decide. Are you deciding to go back to Dallas for my parents' sake, or are you willing to stay… for mine?"

She gave him a side-long glance, her beautiful, chocolate eyes wide with doubt.

With a loud rattle, the front door opened. Kristi waddled in with her husband, Mike, easing the door open for her. "Hi, you two." She made for the stairs.

Dani jumped up. "I'm coming down to you."

She reached to give her a hug. "I didn't know you were coming over."

"Traditional Sunday lunch with the fam." She turned toward Mike. "My hubby."

"Mike Kincaid." He didn't exactly smile but reached over and shook Dani's hand.

"Dani Foster. Nice to finally meet you."

He nodded, then looked up as Dad entered the room.

Jay bristled. Maybe it was purely about-to-be-parent nerves, but his brother-in-law's stiff jaw belied that he'd been talking to Dad. And likely about how Dani had involved Kristi in the murder at the store.

One more wall to break down.

Marji Laine

Dani remained near the new arrivals. Kristi had latched onto her hand and wouldn't let her retreat. Mr. and Mrs. Hunter came into the entry hall to greet them.

If Dani were smart, she'd duck and cover.

Mike Kincaid hugged his mother-in-law. "We passed the sheriff on the way in. He wasn't making trouble again was he?"

Mrs. Hunter uttered a soft, "Oh, dear."

"You could say that." Mr. Hunter shook Mike's hand and pivoted toward the living room. "He just carted Kyle off to jail."

Kristi stumbled. Dani took her arm to steady her. "What are you doing standing around, Dad?"

Mike followed Mr. Hunter into the living room. "For what? Some trumped-up charge based on innuendo and lies?"

Jay's father halted and turned, piercing Dani with a glare. "Perhaps."

She should have escaped while she had the chance.

Jay stepped in front of her. "That's not fair, Dad. She had no idea her statements would implicate Kyle. Maybe you should be more concerned about why he was there at all."

"Are you insinuating that your brother could possibly have had anything to do with that murder?" Mr. Hunter's volume grew with each word.

"Murder!" Kristi flinched, releasing Dani's hand. "Kyle's involved in the murder?"

"How can you think such?" Mr. Hunter turned his glare on his daughter.

His wife stepped between them, her hands on her hips. "Don't you raise your voice to her. You can see how upset she is."

Stricken was the word. One hand rested on her bulging belly and the other stroked her neck.

"*Everyone's* upset at this point." Mr. Hunter once again faced Dani.

"Settle down, Dad." Jay practically growled.

She moved out from behind Jay. Might as well brace herself and take the assault. "I'm okay."

His father began to rant. "I'm sorry, Jay. I know you care for this woman, but she put my daughter and grandson in danger." He shifted his focus to Dani. "You've been spying and eavesdropping, and now you've put my son behind bars."

"*I* didn't kill anyone." How could he blame her for simply reporting what she saw?

"Are you saying that Kyle did?"

Jay put his hand on his father's chest. "You know she didn't mean that. And Kyle's trouble with

Fowler started long before Dani got here."

"Her mentioning those stupid nails sealed Kyle's fate. Had it not been for her statement…."

"No." Kristi advanced and put her hands on her dad's arm. "I told the chief about the nails, too."

"No, precious." Mrs. Hunter drew Kristi away from her angry father. "This is not your fault."

"But it *is* Dani's. Is that it?" Jay folded his arms across his chest and stared down at his father.

Mr. Hunter jutted out his chin. "Neither she nor Kristi would've have been there if Dani hadn't been so nosy."

"They wouldn't have been there if Mom hadn't been sneaking around the shop."

"What?" Mr. Hunter's word was like an explosion. Mrs. Hunter wheeled around and knocked over a glass vase, top-heavy with a silk arrangement. Everyone seemed to lean in until it splintered against the tile floor. Then they burst into more accusations.

Dani backed away. No matter what Jay said,

they would all be better off if she left. His face showed more anger than she'd seen on it, but his father's matched it as they continued to yell. Caught in the middle, Mrs. Hunter alternated between trying to calm her husband and convince her son to back off. Even Mike had entered the fray, obviously fuming over Kristi's unexpected involvement.

Movement in the corner caught her eye. Kristi had flattened her back against the wall. She gripped the door frame with one hand, while pain and surprise etched her face.

Dani hurried to her. The others, tearing into their battle, hadn't seemed to notice her discomfort.

"What's wrong? Is it the baby?

She lifted frightened eyes to Dani's. "I think I'm in labor."

The baby was coming? Now? But it was too early. "You sure?"

Her expression eased. "Oh, yeah. I'm sure."

"Let's get you back to your car." Dani turned

her toward the entrance and raised a shout of her own. "Baby coming. It's delivery time. Dad-to-be, front and center."

The fight halted, turning into a flutter of activity. Mike took Dani's place at his wife's side, and Mrs. Hunter moved to Kristi's other arm. Mr. Hunter took Mike's keys and bolted for the front door.

Jay joined Dani, and they both held back. "Good catch. Again."

"Sometimes the things I see aren't exactly popular." If only she could turn her observation skills off once in a while.

"That's like blaming the traffic camera for a red-light runner." He flipped the lock on the front door as he ushered her to the porch.

"Oh, Jay, no. I can't go to the hospital. Not at a time like this."

"Kristi likes you, hon. She'll want you there. No matter what Mom and Dad say." He paused as they passed Kyle's truck.

"Hang on a minute." Jay opened the driver's side door and ducked inside as Mike's blue minivan, Mr. Hunter at the wheel, pulled down the driveway.

"I knew it. The sheriff was too interested in this cup." Jay withdrew holding the mug in one hand and a packet between two fingers. "Kyle was going to jail today, one way or the other."

Jay poured the white powder down the drain of the outdoor sink. "This time, I'm saving the bag to check for fingerprints." Opening his trunk, he tugged an evidence bag out and dropped the empty plastic inside. "How much you wanna bet this thing is clean of prints?"

Dani got into his truck. "Only if your sheriff's office is humble enough to think they can get caught planting evidence." She grinned as he folded himself into his seat.

"You're right. We'll probably find several

different sets."

"Why does Sheriff Fowler have such a vendetta against your family in the first place?"

He ground his teeth. Ugly story. He started the engine and kicked the A.C. fan into high gear. "Not the whole family. Only Kyle and Dad. Kyle and Fowler's son were best friends in high school until Billy started using. My brother can be a little wild and even stupid, especially when it comes to women. But he's never done drugs. Didn't even flinch when I flushed the packet we'd found the other night."

"So Billy got caught?"

Jay nodded. That had been the rub. Kyle hadn't been involved, but Fowler was sure he'd thrown his son out in order to save his own behind. "Dad's office raided a party at the park. The deputies expected to find underage drinkers. Instead, they nailed Billy as a pusher."

"No wonder his dad got so mad."

"Yeah. Unreasonable, but a parent is likely to

believe their kid even when the evidence says they're wrong." He'd seen it over and over in Dallas during arrests and also in court. "Attack the innocent stranger in order to protect the guilty son."

"Not unlike the way your dad has attacked me." Dani squirmed in her seat. "I don't know everything that's going on, Jay, but your parents are hurting. It's easier to take out their frustration on me, a stranger, than it is to accept the responsibility for the problems and mistakes."

"I know. I can't excuse it, though." He stroked the tendril of soft hair that had escaped her loose ponytail. "You're precious to me. Naturally, I'm going to defend you. Especially when you haven't done anything wrong."

"Not against your mom and dad." She turned toward him and clutched his hand, taking a deep breath. "I don't want to come between you."

"Then don't leave. Let them get to know you." A whisper of hope threaded through his chest.

She held his gaze, but her eyes registered

doubt. "I suppose, if you're sure about this, I'm willing to try again. But I have to say, they seemed bent on my absence. How do you propose to change their minds about that?"

"You're going to stay, then?" The tightness in his gut eased.

"For a while, I guess. You did kidnap my suitcase." She smirked. "Not like I have much of a choice."

He laughed, enjoying the feel of it after the thick tension inside the house.

"But… if I'm going to stay here, I need to earn your parents' respect somehow." She tapped her chin several times with her forefinger and let her gaze wander across the roof liner.

"You're not thinking of snooping around this murder." Fowler would haul her to the county lock up.

"We can't leave Kyle in jail. And investigating is a strength for both of us."

Jay winced. "And jurisdiction? I know you

understand that concept."

She waved away his comment. "We're going to get to the bottom of this." The fire in her eyes worried him.

"That's a crime scene, Dani."

"You're a crime scene investigator, last time I checked." She shot him a side-long look.

"I'm not in the habit of breaking and entering." Not to mention crossing a police tape. But how could he allow the sheriff to railroad his brother into a jail cell without at least attempting to build a defense?

"Are you willing to trust Chief Harris and that county overlord to solve this crime correctly?"

Nothing simple about that question. His family rested on one side of the scales and his career on the other. "What you're suggesting could land us both in jail."

"Or could get Kyle out." She turned to face the windshield. "I'm sure the locals are watching the place. We would need to wait until tonight."

Reckless plan. Not to mention against the law. Jay shifted into gear and coasted down the long driveway.

Dad had always had a good relationship with Chief Harris. Maybe he could ask for permission, on Jay's behalf, to examine the scene. That risked a negative response, but at least anything they found could be used in court to defend his brother. "I'll talk to Dad."

The conversation wouldn't be an easy one, but then nothing had been exactly easy about this trip.

Chapter Twelve

The facts were simple. Basalind had been murdered. Someone had killed him. There had to be evidence left at the scene. Unless the police had collected every possible piece. Doubtful.

Dani let Jay drive in silence, mulling over all that she'd seen during the fire. Not that she remembered much more than the burning body and the falling ceiling tiles.

Jay pulled into a spot in the Emergency Room lot at the regional hospital and opened his door. "Should I wait for you here?" Dani unbuckled her seatbelt as Jay ran around the car. Hopefully he'd let her stay where she was. The last thing Mr. and Mrs. Hunter needed was another emotional distraction.

God, I've been nothing but a source of conflict between Jay and his parents. Please don't let my presence here start another fight.

He opened the door and held out his hand. "Of course not." His soft expression and the gentle way he took her hand told his feelings. He had to know the turmoil her presence would again visit on the family. But his eyes held deep sincerity. The love he'd been stating to her over the past few days poured out. He helped her from the car and held her close. "I love my family. I wish they were behaving more like themselves. But their decisions and opinions and actions have no effect on how I feel about you."

His eyes lingered on her mouth and she reached for his kiss. Mmm, soft and soothing. Then he pulled her close so that her head rested against his chin. "I can only hope that their attitudes won't affect how you feel about me."

How she felt? Part balloon; part lead. One moment she longed to proclaim her love. The next, she felt she'd do nothing but sink him into a mire of lies and desperation. She shoved aside the heavy half and relished the delight of his nearness, letting his fingertips drift across her back and down her arms. "I so wanted them to like me, Jay, but they don't. It doesn't change how much I care about you, but I worry that I'm driving you away from your family."

"You're not driving anything." He wrapped his arms around her and gave her a squeeze. "I know my folks will come around when their stress subsides."

She wasn't so sure, but when he released her, she took his offered hand and joined him as he went into the building. Kristi and Mike had disappeared, but Mr. and Mrs. Hunter sat near the doors that went back to the Labor/Delivery area.

"How is she?" Jay called to them as he and

Dani approached. Mr. Hunter stood but wouldn't look at her. He wouldn't look at his son either, for that matter.

"It's bona fide labor." Mrs. Hunter lifted a quivering smile and reddened eyes in their direction. "She's in a lot of pain, but she chewed us out all the way here."

"Pain talking?" Jay sat in seats across from them and pulled Dani down beside him.

Mr. Hunter also sat. His eyes had a drippy appearance as well, almost like his wife's, but his deep tan didn't show any redness around them. "No. More like bitter disappointment... in us." He looked up, glancing first at Jay and then at Dani. "You have to understand that we were only trying to protect our family."

A cold hand crept down Dani's spine. "From me?" He'd been sheriff. Still had all sorts of connections. Had he investigated her? Found out more than he should know?

"From revelation of some things that... well,

that we're ashamed of." He glanced at his wife, then turned back to face her and Jay. "I suppose Jay has explained about my retirement."

"Dad, don't go into all that here." Jay looked around and tilted his head toward a couple of older women seated behind them and to one side.

Mr. Hunter followed the gesture and lifted his chin. "Ah. Good thought. But the details aside, we viewed you, Dani, as a risk to the secrets we were hiding. Your arrival was untimely, through no fault of your own. Then you happened to catch me in a heated conversation with a man of questionable character."

"Poor at best." Mrs. Hunter stared at the floor, but her comment had enough volume to carry.

Jay's dad patted his wife's knee and continued. "You did see Caroline outside of the store yesterday. Another reason for us to be wary of you, even suspect that you were intentionally here to hurt Jay and our family."

Tears burned the back of Dani's eyes. How

they must hate her. "I'd never do that." Not intentionally, but weren't her own secrets going to take Jay to the same end?

Mr. Hunter swallowed. "Kristi… made me realize…." His wife nudged him and he glanced her way. "Made us realize that we've not treated you kindly. Not at all." His gaze settled on her. "We've disrespected Jay. We've prejudged you." He shook his head. "I can't go into all of the details. We felt we had to guard ourselves."

"I even wanted to cancel the Fourth Festival." Mrs. Hunter's worried look traveled from Dani to Jay and back.

Mr. Hunter studied his hands in his lap. "I've never wanted to live as a pretender. Never had the need to lie and hide things to save face."

"Not normal for our family either." Jay's comment held a sting, though he couldn't know how he'd pricked her heart.

Dani studied the carpet. Lying, hiding, secrets. They were all such a huge part of her life now. Far be it for her to hurl rocks. "I understand how my presence must have been a burden. Especially with regard to my curious nature. I confess, it takes over sometimes. I'm so sorry to have caused you such concern."

"You have nothing to apologize for, Dani." Mrs. Hunter leaned forward from her cushioned seat, making the vinyl squeak. "Nothing you have done would have given us a moment of worry had it not been for our already heightened alert."

"It's okay, Mom." Jay sighed and patted her hand. He stood. "I even told Dani that nothing usually bothers you. Not even something like the garden gate."

His mom lifted her gaze to the ceiling and clasped her hands. "I was so distracted by the fight. That gate wasn't your responsibility, Dani, and… and I'm ashamed for fussing at you, dear. I haven't done anything like that before. Not ever. Well, except to my own kids."

Jay rubbed his hip. "I can testify to that." He

chuckled and wrapped his arm around his mom. "Please don't stress over this. You're about to be a grandma. And Dani and I are okay. Right?" He glanced at her.

"Absolutely." She mustered a smile she didn't feel.

Mr. Hunter gave her one in response. "I'd appreciate it if you would allow us to start over."

"Of course, but your circumstances haven't changed, have they?" Wouldn't they still feel wary of her?

"No." He stood and paced a few steps before turning back toward Dani. "But our hearts have. Jay would not have brought you here on a flight of fantasy. The fact that you came to meet his family speaks value into your character as well."

"And the fact that you have stayed even through all of our rude and inconsiderate behavior." His wife moved to his side and tucked her hand into the crook of his arm. "The very least we can do is offer you hospitality. The most is to treat you like one of the family."

Mr. Hunter patted his wife's hand. "And we intend to do both. Once we know the extent of Kristi's situation, we'll sit down with you and let both of you know all that is happening."

Jay's jaw dropped. "Both of us?"

"I'm sorry son. There are things I still...." Mr. Hunter looked down.

His wife took up the statement. "Your father is a good man. A good husband. A noble defender."

A nurse came in. "Kincaid?"

"Yes." Mrs. Hunter whirled around.

"Are you Kristi's parents?" The young woman lifted her eyebrows with the question. Receiving a nod, she opened the automatic door with her key. "Follow me."

"We'll be taking care of a few things, Dad. Be back later." Jay offered his hand to Dani. "That wasn't so bad, was it?"

"No, except you didn't ask him to talk to Chief Harris."

He nodded. "The more I think about it, the more I believe I can persuade the chief to let us take a look at the scene. We're all on the same team, you know."

"Not exactly. We're not on the sheriff's team at all." Not that she'd want to be. Seemed like that man was dirty from his socks upward. "Maybe we should get Kyle's take on all of this."

"I was thinking the same thing. He said he didn't kill Basalind, and we have to believe that."

"And yet, it's likely he was the man who ran from the building." If he didn't commit the murder, Dani didn't like the other, most probable, option.

"We don't have anything to lose, and speaking to him would be the first thing I'd do if this were my case." He turned onto a highway that led out of town.

Dani's mind wandered. What had Mrs. Hunter been doing at the StopNShop? Could she have murdered the owner? Everything in her denied that possibility. Especially with her own son in jail. No, she would have confessed right away.

In fact, Dani half-expected Mr. Hunter to admit to the killing simply to force Kyle's release. Hopefully she and Jay could make some headway on the mystery before his parents were tempted to do something so foolish.

The trip to the county seat took the better part of an hour. The sheriff almost laughed when he heard their request and made them wait for almost two more.

When he finally approached, he brought along one of his deputies with him. "Still clearing some details up. I have an errand." He pointed to the man. "Deputy Rodgers will keep you informed of the progress."

With a smirk the man strolled from the building. Jay eyed the deputy. "He doesn't have any intention of allowing us to see my brother, does he?"

In silence, the man strolled to a nearby window and glanced through the blinds. After a moment, he returned, scanning the virtually empty room as he came. He eyed the dispatcher in the far corner, but the woman was on the phone. "Sorry. His only goal is to see how long he can keep you hanging around here."

Dani pressed to standing, resisting the groan her aching knees urged. "Ooh, that man."

Jay clasped her hand. "He's bent on hurting my family. No reason why he should do anything remotely nice."

The deputy escorted them outside. "Wish I could help you, but I rather like my job."

"I understand."

"Liked it a lot better when your dad was in charge, though." The man hesitated. "I can tell you this much. Kyle told the sheriff that he'd been inside the building. That Basalind had been stabbed and was already dead. Sheriff thinks Kyle started the fire, but your brother clammed-up, then."

He probably should have clammed-up earlier. If the sheriff hadn't already thought to accuse Mrs.

Hunter, he had plenty of reason to do so at this point.

"Thanks. Please let him know that we were here. And that I'm calling an attorney friend of mine." Jay pulled out his phone.

"I can do that." The deputy gave a quick wave and stepped back inside.

Jay moved to the shade of a huge tree laden with clusters of green pods. "Barry Dyson is a good guy. Met him in college, and we sort of worked against each other for a while in Dallas. Then he moved out here to help his dad."

He turned his attention to the phone. "Hey. No, I'm not in trouble. But my brother is." He smoothed his hair back as he listened. A low voice seeped from his phone, but Dani couldn't distinguish any of the words.

What a good brother. Even without knowing all that had been going on, Jay was dedicated to doing his best for Kyle.

"He's here, in High Grove."

Seemed a nice town. Not nearly the size of Dallas, but plenty big. Hard to get past the creepy sheriff, though.

"I know it's Sunday, but I thought you might have sway, especially with the flimsy evidence they're using." Jay squeezed his eyes shut. "Murder. Fowler didn't give details, just Mirandized him and stuck him in the back of his car."

Jay opened his eyes and sought hers. "Thanks. I miss dad being sheriff, too. I'll let him know you said so, but I'm not sure he'd take such a comment from a defense attorney as a compliment." Jay's laugh warmed her heart.

He asked his friend to do what he could and hung up with a shrug. "I've done everything I know how to do."

"Have you prayed?"

He winced. "Oh, man. Should have been first thing." He took her hands and bowed his head over the hood of the truck asking for guidance, help, and justice for Kyle and for his dad. "We're not in control, God. Help us realize that and be okay with it."

After the amen, she looked in his eyes. "Must be tough for a cop to not be in control."

"Technically, I'm never really in control, right? Can't force my heart to beat or my lungs to pump. Can't even change the weather."

"But you know who can." She squeezed his hands and reached to kiss his cheek.

"That I do."

He called his mom to check on Kristi and took down a dinner order for all of them, especially since no one had even had lunch. By the time they finished their errands and dinner with Jay's folks, sunset approached.

Jay told her what he knew of his parents' situation as they left the hospital again, heading toward town. She'd not been shocked about the revelation of the gambling. Issues like that could happen to anyone. Being Christian didn't make one immune to temptation. Her past few years bore that out. "I'm sorry your dad became embroiled in that. It's an addiction just like alcohol, pornography, even food."

"Sweetheart, I know they didn't mean to take out their stress on you." He pulled to the back of the StopNShop and turned off his lights. Covering her hand with his, he searched her face. "I'm certain their apology was sincere."

"I'm positive you're right. I... I hope that they'll like me better this time." What were the chances? She was still nosy... still opened her mouth at the worst possible times.

He squeezed her hand. "You'll see. Stay here. I'm going across the street to talk to Chief Harris."

She stared at the back door of the store. "But there isn't any police tape up."

He turned and looked. "Still, I don't want you in there alone."

"So you want me to sit out here alone? In this sketch area?"

"This is a little town." He chuckled. "Run down areas, yeah. But nothing around here is sketch. No gangs. Little crime. You're safe."

"As safe as I'd be inside."

He started to respond, but she held up her flat palm. "And if I'm inside *with* your permission, I can use a set of your gloves to make sure I'm not messing with any would-be evidence if there is anything to find."

Closing his eyes, he let a heavy exhale escape. "Wear a mask."

"You got it."

He opened the console between their seats and pulled out a fresh pair of latex gloves and a surgeon's mask still inside the plastic wrapper.

"You should use these at every scene, you know."

"Claustrophobic." He snickered.

"Yeah, right." She stepped down from the truck and slipped the items on.

"You've got your phone in case you find

anything?" Jay reached for her hand.

"Got it." Though the mask muffled her answer.

He bent to kiss her through the mask.

"You missed." Not by much, but she couldn't resist the tease.

He lifted it with his finger. "Not this time." His mouth found hers with a little more passion than she expected in the dark, downtown lot of a little town. As his kiss deepened, she pulled off the mask entirely and wrapped her arms around his neck, reveling in the confirmation of his love.

They finally separated, both breathing hard.

Jay pulled the mask from her hand and slipped it over her head. "I think this thing should stay in place better than that."

She giggled and adjusted the straps.

He took a step away but pointed back toward her.

"And I'll be careful." She saluted and turned toward the black opening of the store. Pulling out her phone, she flicked to her flashlight app and shined it around the entrance. All that remained of the police tape was a torn piece dangling from one side. Certainly not against the law to enter. Public place, wide open entrance. Not even any caution tape as a result of the fire. At least, that would be her justification if someone should ask.

The fire hadn't been allowed to get much further along than the aisle in which it started. The ceiling above that area was missing all of the tiles, leaving the blackened frame to stand out like a skinless skeleton against the metal roof. Besides that, everything else had remained intact.

Certainly not the damage she'd expected from what felt like a firestorm.

Something skittered across the floor.

Dani jumped and almost dropped her phone. *Calm.* She'd not get any investigating done if she flinched at every sound. Avoiding the dead man's aisle, she made her way to the center of the store.

The checkout counter was a horseshoe of cabinets with a hinged bar to the back to complete a solid oval. The surface had a line of convenience food warmers along the back side. The hotdog cooker was empty, but one machine held a pretzel and another held a several paper bowls of tortilla chips. A nacho machine stood next to the glass case.

The area facing the front glass had a myriad of product displays covering half of the side. The other half, where there should've been cash registers, was empty. The police had probably confiscated them. She eyed the two low shelves under the bare counter. Some file folders, paper bowls, popcorn boxes, cups, a board full of keys, rolls of register tape, boxes of plastic bags, and a kitchen cleaner that had likely never been used.

Dani moved aside a display of cigarettes and another of gum. Nothing interesting there, though next to them, a large terra cotta, rectangular pot looked out of place. Sort of like a window-box planter without the plants. Instead, various seed packets were crammed into the holder. Dani let her fingers walk through the packets: watermelon, sunflower, bluebonnets, poppies, and more. Why would something like this be in a convenience store?

Wedged between the packets, she found change, a tiny pocket knife, a hearing aid battery, and even a couple of earrings. She eyed the diamond stud, wondering if it was real. Probably not. The other was a loop with little beads of crystal and sapphire. Obviously items that people had lost.

So first, why were there seeds in a place like this? And second, why did anyone actually look through them or get close enough to drop their possessions?

She shoved the planter, but it wouldn't budge. Pushing again, she used more of her body weight to no avail. Setting down her phone, she tried to lift the thing. The boards of the counter creaked. This wasn't simply heavy. It was attached.

Grabbing her phone, she examined the base of the planter. Al fresco swirls and embellishments adorned the outside. Lots of crevices and crannies in the texture, but nothing that seemed out of place. No section moved like a hidden button or panel. She removed some of the seed packets from the inside. The inside was very shallow compared to the depth of the large planter. There had to be a hidden panel in there somewhere. She continued to pull out the packets and other items, leaving them on the linoleum counter top. Having emptied the holder, she shined her light from one edge to the other. No buttons. Nothing looked out of kilter at all for that matter, except the paint on one end seemed faded.

Faded? On the inside? She pressed against the discolored area and something gave ever-so-slightly. She pushed again, and the entire edge moved outward about an inch. An exposed metal bar showed a lock.

She took her light to the board she'd seen. A slew of random keys hung on each hook. She pulled all of the keys off the first ring and tried them one at a time. None worked. She took the two keys from the next hook and lifted the pile from the third place as well.

The first one fit into the lock, and it clicked when she turned it.

"Oh, yeah." She set the rest of them on the bare counter, then inspected the planter. Strange. Nothing had opened.

This was ridiculous. The planter had unused space. Even the counter had a good six extra inches to its top. She squinted and ran her fingers over the back side of that extra wide section of shelf.

"Ouch." Her fingernail bent backward at a jagged edge. She shined her light. That wasn't a jagged edge. It was a tiny door that had unlatched. The button lever inside released the entire back panel of the shelf. She lifted it like a library shelf and slid the cover into a gap, then gasped at the contents of the compartment.

Drugs all right, but that wasn't the only thing there.

Marji Laine

Chapter Thirteen

Jay flashed his badge at the officer attending the front desk. "Is the chief available?" He'd come much later than he'd planned.

"Let me check." She smiled, showing straight white teeth against her darker complexion. She turned away and spoke into a Bluetooth apparatus on her ear. After a moment, she turned back to him. "He'll see you, Sergeant Hunter."

A door opened on his right, and he entered the employee area. A couple of benches hugged a half-wall that surrounded five desks. Only two of these were occupied at the moment. The receptionist pointed to a door with milky glass against the back wall. "He's waiting for you."

That was a good sign. The man opened his office door as Jay neared and extended his dark hand. "Hunter. Good to see you again in a not-so-official capacity. Or is it?" The man wore a pleasant expression, but his eyes plainly belied that Jay had been expected.

"Semi-official." He took the chair the chief indicated, and the man closed his office door. "Sheriff Fowler locked up my brother for Basalind's murder."

The man's eyebrows lowered the tiniest bit. Dad had always said that Harris was the most unflappable lawman he'd ever worked with.

"Happened several hours ago. How come you didn't know about the arrest?"

Harris's face turned into a cement mask with no emotion of any sort. "You're positive of your facts?"

"I was there. Tried to see him, but Fowler

wouldn't let me in."

"You've no jurisdiction." The chief sat in the large chair behind his desk.

"Fully aware. And I know you and your team know your job. But I'm a crime scene specialist. My girl has solved several crimes herself. Her observation skills are outstanding."

"Be that as it may…."

Jay intended to get his entire request out. "I'm only asking for a tiny bit of latitude here. Some inter-office cooperation."

"To get your brother off." Harris lifted one eyebrow.

"To see that justice is done." Jay took a breath. "I'm convinced Kyle is innocent, Chief, but I'll be the first one to want him to serve time if I find out I'm wrong. I don't want to find evidence to prove his innocence. I only want to make sure there isn't anything left out. Good or bad." *Please, let Kyle be innocent.* His parents would disown him if he found something that cemented the case against his brother, but that was the chance he had to take.

"You know, Hunter, I'm pretty proud of you. Proud that you did ride-alongs with your dad. Proud that you helped out around here when you were in school."

"Citizen patrol." A half-grin spread across Jay's face.

"Yeah. Best one we had when you were organizing it." The chief leaned forward. "But my staff is good. Just because you're big-city now doesn't mean you're any better."

"I'm not a better man, and I'm not a better cop than any you have serving. But how many murders do you deal with in a year?"

His mouth clamped shut.

"I have to be better at collecting evidence, simply from sheer repetition. Thirty-two crime scenes last month, and June was rather light." He leaned forward. "I'm not trying to show up your team, Chief Harris. I'm desperate, and I truly believe I can help."

The man's exhale sounded rather like a growl. He rocked back and sighed again. "I suppose you can join the team tomorrow when we finish the sweep. But only to observe and point out anything they might be missing. Your girl can come through after we've finished."

No, that wasn't right. "After you finish? You're not done already?"

"All right, Speedy. We *don't* have all the bells and whistles here in Podunk that you have in the big city. We actually have to take measurements and collect samples the old fashioned way. And with a scene like this, brother, let me tell you there is plenty to be had."

"Yes. No. I mean, I thought you had completed your work, already."

"When we finish, we'll remove the crime scene tape. Or does your team move so fast it doesn't need to seal off an area." He smirked.

Jay stood. "Come on, Chief. And bring one of your officers." He opened the door.

"Just a second, there, Hunter. What are you all up in arms about?" His footsteps followed Jay into the hall.

Turning, Jay clutched at the man's upper arm. "Your crime tape's already gone." He whirled and rushed toward the front of the building, the sheriff's loud voice calling for an assist.

He'd left Dani in danger. Again.

Dani stared at the stacks of money. Next to them was a line of medium-sized, brown envelopes. There had to be at least two dozen of the thick mailers standing on the shelf and another several lying flat on top of them. She picked up one that hadn't been closed entirely and shifted the flap around the closure. Inside were photos of a woman in an indecent situation. Make that several indecent situations, and with several different men.

"Blackmail?" Shoving the contents back inside, she replaced the envelope exactly as it had been. If each held the life of a different person hostage to their past, no wonder Basalind was dead.

A car's tires crunched across the gravel outside. Lights careened off the walls toward her. Jay was on foot. Though the chief could have driven back, she turned off her phone app as a precaution. Ducking, she reached to remove the key and shove the planter closed. Several seed packets slipped off the counter, along with some of the other items she'd found. All of it smacked or clanged onto the tile. *Shhh*.

Footsteps sounded in the gravel. Slow ones. Great. A drug-pusher coming for his stash, and she knelt beside its hiding place. Her breath against the mask sounded like a Darth Vader impression. She tugged the paper off and tossed it to the ground. Crouching lower, she leaned on one hand. Something on the ground jabbed it. She swallowed her outcry and picked up the injuring item.

Memory flooded back as the hollow sound of a woman's high heel on linoleum echoed through the room.

The earring. All very blue and white like Lauren always wore. Dani had admired something similar on the night of the dinner party. The event in a house not thirty yards away. Might not have been the same hoop earring, but if it was, what was it doing in a place Lauren had never been? She'd left to take that call. Was gone for at least twenty minutes, though Dani couldn't remember if she'd had both earrings when she'd returned.

But whether the woman sneaking into the store was Lauren or not, the murder had to be about the drugs or the envelopes.

As silently as possible, she pulled out the cover and pressed it closed, then covered the panel over the button.

Another step sounded on the linoleum, and a light swept the room.

Tucking the key into her pocket, Dani duck-walked toward the opening in the u-shaped counter. Something skittered across the floor in her direction. She swallowed her terror.

Whoever it was at the back door let out a sharp scream. Dani used the distraction to scoot under the bar. She put her back to the counter and faced the front glass, gently settling one knee on the ground and biting her lip against the pain. In full view of the front of the store, she was somewhat hidden from the back. And in perfect cover from the person when they reached the counter.

Except for the mirrors. She'd forgotten about those. She could see herself in one convex glass as the intruder came into view. Definitely female and with pale hair, she could be Lauren, though positive identification was impossible.

Hopefully the woman wouldn't glance up at the mirror. Dani kept her eyes on the reflection, though, as the woman slowed and shone the light around the room. Dani slipped her phone out and turned the sound off, then pressed in a 911 text to Jay. She glanced back at the reflection.

Suddenly a light burst into her face where the

woman had shined it into the mirror. "Hello, Dani." Lauren's voice all right.

Dani pressed her back to the counter.

Lauren lifted a 9mm in her other hand. "I thought you might get nosy enough to come over here. Especially after I heard the rest of the family was at the hospital. Last place you want to be. Am I right?" Her laughter sounded forced.

"I'm nosy. Remember?" Lauren hadn't heard anything about her real job.

She chuckled. "According to Kristi, you are the most fabulous, unofficial crime scene investigator that Dallas has to offer. And I need you to find some things for me."

So she'd taken down the crime scene tape to lure Dani inside. Dani flattened her lips, hating to be so predictable.

The light moved a bit to the left but stayed on the opposite side of the counter. It danced over the planter. "I bet you've already found what I'm looking for." She aimed the light at the mirror again. "Where is it?"

"I only just noticed the planter before you arrived." She eyed the closest aisle. The one that had been Basalind's resting place. That was her *only* escape option? Really?

"Well, then you are no help at all." She aimed the gun in Dani's direction and began to circle the counter, all the while keeping the light trained on the mirror. "I've got my eye on you." She giggled, a sickly, humorless sound.

Another step, and she'd be almost directly under the mirror. She'd have to abandon watching Dani at that point. But she was also cutting off the escape route that Dani had planned. The back door was the only other option, but there was too much open space between the counter and the gaping exit.

Dani wouldn't make that even at a full-tilt run.

"What's your play, Dani?"

Jay's sprint for the store was halted by an

eighteen-wheeler taking its time on the narrow street. "Come on, already."

The chief put his hand on Jay's shoulder. "Maybe you should stay here." He had to shout to be heard of the truck's chug. "You have no jurisdiction, remember?"

"My girl. Dani is inside." Jay slapped at the crawling trailer. "No tape." The truck slowed. Jay punched at it again and ran behind the tail with the chief in his tracks. He paused to let a pickup go by from the other direction, then ran across.

A light danced through the window. Jay paused on the outer edge of the lot. Far enough away to see but not be seen.

"Your girl has a gun?" Harris and another officer stopped nearby.

"No." But clearly someone did. It caught the beam as the light moved from side to side.

Jay's stomach knotted. "I'm going to the back."

"You still don't...."

"Yeah, yeah. Jurisdiction." He didn't stay to hear anymore. An odd vehicle was in the back, next to his truck. Oldsmobile. He'd not seen one like that since high school. He paused at the truck to collect his weapon. Stupid of him not to have it in the first place. Then, avoiding the gravel, he jogged the perimeter of the lot and crept in on the grass patches nearest the back wall of the store.

"Your move, Dani." A woman? Lauren?

The knot tightened. With no idea what was going on, his girl was in danger. Of that he was sure.

The time for her decision had come. Dani ducked under the bar into the center of the oval as Lauren jumped beyond the opposite one. The explosion of her gun shocked Dani for a second, and wood splintered on the other side where she had huddled a moment before. Needing a distraction, she inched closer to the center of the counter, behind the candy rack that rose like stadium seating. She eyed the heavy hot dog cooker a few feet from her. This had to work. Leaping to her feet, she shoved the candy display over with all the force she could muster.

Something crashed through the front window at that same moment. The gun went off again, filling the room with its blast, and more glass broke.

"Dani." Jay's voice was behind her. He'd be silhouetted at the back entrance.

She lurched for the cooker and wheeled around where Lauren stood poised to shoot through the back door. Another earsplitting shot rang out. With all her momentum, Dani heaved the heavy piece, catching Lauren in her right temple.

Someone kicked in part of the window. "Lift your hands and identify yourself." Whoever was entering lifted a new light, much brighter than Lauren's, that blinded her.

"I'm Dani Foster." She raised her hands. *Lord, please don't let Lauren get another shot off at this point.* "I don't have a weapon. She does." She pointed in Lauren's general direction.

Immediately, the light moved to the floor on the other side of the counter. Lauren lay on her side, a gash on her head. No sign of her gun, but both of her hands were visible. The hotdog cooker, smashed to indiscernible scraps, had slid to the edge of another aisle.

Another light joined the first, again making her squint. Where was Jay?

Jay froze with his gun in ready position. He'd only shot one other person before. *God, please don't let me have killed that woman.* The chief's voice calling for hands to be raised gave Jay some welcome relief. No shots in response was even better.

An officer joined Jay at the back door. "Surrender your weapon, sir."

"Jay Hunter, Dallas Police." Still clutching the

grip of his gun with his thumb, he lifted both hands, fingers wide. "Perp inside aimed a gun at me."

"Face the wall." The officer approached Jay with his gun aimed.

Great. *Let's just add humiliation to this visit.* Not to mention some woman could be dying on the floor in there. He slowly turned, keeping his hands skyward. "You need to call an ambulance."

"Already done." As an answer, a siren revved up not too far from their location. The young man pulled Jay's gun out of his hand. "Hands on the wall. Spread your feet."

He had to be kidding. "Check my wallet. My badge is in there. Back pocket."

"Hands on the wall." The man was nothing if not persistent.

With a growl, Jay assumed the position.

The officer patted Jay down. "Dallas credentials don't hold weight here, sir." But he pulled out his wallet, anyway. "Sergeant. You can turn around, now."

Still, Jay moved slowly. "Can I have my weapon back?" He looked down at the young cop, probably barely out of training. "No, sir. Not without Chief Harris's okay."

Jay cracked a half smile. "Good answer." He glanced at the cop's nameplate. "Appleby. Kin to Daniel Appleby?"

"My older brother." He lifted his chin and handed Jay his wallet.

"You're Cole? Really?" The kid only stood as high as Jay's chest when he'd left. "Your brother used to help me on my grandfather's farm."

"I remember. And your dad was sheriff for all those years. Sure do miss having him in that position."

Not as much as Jay did. "Now can I have my weapon back?"

The kid shook his head. "No, sir."

Chief Harris came through the door, shoving Dani in front of him by her upper arm.

Her eyes lit when she spotted Jay, and she

threw her arms around his neck. "Oh, Jay. I didn't know what happened to you."

"Are you all right? I heard the shots."

"I saw you in the doorway. She could have killed you." She pressed her lips against his, sending electricity all through him. Even if she couldn't say the words, she must love him a little.

"All right, you two." Harris reclaimed Dani's arm and urged them both away from the door. "We need to iron all of this out over at the station."

"Wait." Dani pulled back. "I have to show you what this is about. At least, I think it's about blackmail."

Even in the dim light, the chief's eyes squinted.

"I thought it was drug pushing." Jay followed Dani through the gaping hole. EMTs had reached Lauren. As Jay entered, they lifted her onto a stretcher, though they continued to work on her. Their flood lights lit the entire room, particularly a broad spread of blood under the gurney.

"I thought so, too." She paused behind the

counter. Still wearing her latex gloves, she fished a key from her pocket. "I found this on a board on the lower shelf."

Jay couldn't see any lock, until she pressed out the end of a rectangular planter. His jaw dropped as she revealed each step. "Everything in here is exactly as I found it." She lifted the side panel and shoved it in.

Harris whistled. "All this time, I've believed Sheriff Fowler's claim that this site was a counterfeit to distract from the real site they hadn't found yet." He turned to Appleby. "Run back to the station for the crime scene kit. Bring Connors back with you. And one of you call Mrs. Jessup to come photograph all of this."

"Yes, sir." The man was already running before he finished his response.

"Since you have the gloves, suppose you fill me in on what all this is in here." Harris waved his palm toward the brown envelopes, most of them rather fat.

Marji Laine

"I only checked one of them." She took one of about a half-dozen that lay on top of the upright ones. "The clasp is broken on this one, so I could get a look without breaking into it."

"Oh, that makes it all better." Harris's statement dripped with sarcasm.

"Without her, you wouldn't have even found all of this." There had to be tens of thousands of dollars' worth of drugs in the clear bins next to the bookended envelopes and the wrapped piles of money.

"Duly noted." He moved closer to peer over Dani's shoulder.

She pulled out a stack of pictures.

Mayor Cambridge's wife seemed to be the principal character, but Jay also recognized one of the school board members. "Well, that's disturbing."

"Lucrative for the one who had them." Harris backed away. "That the only one you saw?"

"Yes, sir." Dani repacked the envelope. "I

barely had enough time to get this all closed again before Lauren came inside."

Hard to believe Lauren was involved in something like this. "Chief, was Lauren…?"

"Out cold." He glanced at Jay. "You only winged her, boy. What do they teach you at that big city department?"

"Well, she had been little more than a shadow behind the flashlight."

Harris waved off his excuse. "Your girl here belted her with something."

"A hotdog cooker." Dani's dimple came out of hiding.

"That's gonna leave a mark." Jay smiled at her. *Thank You, God, that I didn't kill her. And thank You for protecting Dani. Again.*

The chief laughed. "Probably permanent, but I don't see that as something she can plea-bargain with. I saw her shooting. Dani can testify to that as well."

"Uh…." Her smile fell off. "I doubt you'll

need me. She wanted to know where all of this was. I bet you'll find something in one of those envelopes that will implicate her."

Jay put his arm around her shoulders. Still with the secrets. "We'll work it out."

Though he'd added a vein of assurance in his words, he said them as much to convince himself as to comfort her. With all the things she continued to hide from him, could they ever have a future together?

Chapter Fourteen

Tick-tock.

Dani shifted on the hard bench and stared at the black and white clock, the only decoration on the wall of the police department waiting room. Well, beyond a plaque proclaiming the championship of some softball tournament.

Watching the little red bar click around the circle, she counted off another minute. Had they really been sitting there for another two hours? What was with these rural policemen?

She leaned against Jay's shoulder and watched the red bar on another trek around the dial.

"Chief, can we leave?" Jay pulled his arm from around her shoulders and rubbed it. The hard bench had caused it to fall asleep twice already, poor guy.

Dani shifted her position. "Seriously, we've told you all we can."

Harris poked his head through the doorway of an office toward the end of a short hallway. "Come on back."

Ugh. More questions? She'd already told him about the earring, the dinner party, and how she'd come to be inside the store moment by moment. What more could he ask.

Jay ushered her inside and let her have the single seat. "We need to get to the hospital."

"I know all about Kristi. Still in labor. Doing fine."

That was good to know.

"Thought, since you've been so helpful, maybe you'd like to see what Lauren Stiles was worried about." He held up a stack of photos, his gloves making slight squeaks against the prints.

Jay glanced at Dani then back to the chief. "Last thing I want to see is Lauren's indiscretions."

Last thing she wanted him to see, as well.

"Oh, you'll want to take a look at this." He spread the photos out on the desk. "Basalind liked fishing as much as he liked…"

"…making money." Jay finished with him. "Yeah. Heard that before."

"Seems he took these from his boat. Found a really nice zoom lens with a Canon in his apartment, but we didn't make a connection, then."

The pictures were clearly of Lauren, much younger. In one, she was tying a rope to a cinder block. "What is she doing?"

The chief handed Dani a magnifying glass. "Oh, my gosh. That's a body."

"She threw a body into the lake?" Jay squinted at another photo.

"More like rolled. More than ten years ago by the looks of the bridge construction behind her. Southside Bridge over Bender Lake." He pushed another photo forward. "Recognize the car?"

Dani shifted to the other view. A bright yellow VW bug sat behind the young version of Lauren. She leaned over someone on the pavement.

"Yeah. She drove it all through high school." Jay swallowed. "You telling me she killed someone?"

"Hard to say. The way the construction was back then. Coulda been an accident. Or she coulda been cleaning up for someone else." Chief Harris accepted the glass back from Dani and handed it to Jay. "Check out the front of the car."

Jay scanned the photo. "Looks like a dent in the fender there."

"Who's the dead guy?" Dani leaned over Jay's shoulder.

"Not sure. Might be a vagrant." The chief used tweezers to slip the photos into a plastic baggie. "We'll know more when—if—we find the body."

Jay straightened. "From the photos, it looks like Lauren hit the guy. Whether or not it was an accident, only Lauren can tell us."

Chief Harris stacked up several plastic bags. "Her car sort of disappeared sometime around then. Before she left town, she started driving around her daddy's Oldsmobile." The chief glanced between the two of them.

"Oldsmobile. That's where I'd seen that car before. The one parked behind the StopNShop. It belonged to Mr. Stiles." Jay looked at the chief who nodded.

The chief collected the glass from Dani. "So now you know the why behind all of this."

Not all of it. "Doesn't work, Chief." Dani stood, tapped her fingertips together, and turned to the man's cluttered wall. News clippings, color-book pictures, photos of the elementary kids with some dog mascot. "Why now?" She turned. "For all I can tell, she's successful, dresses in fashion, wears expensive jewelry and perfume, so paying the blackmail hasn't hurt her."

"How do we know Basalind didn't just hit her

up to start paying?" Harris's eyes narrowed.

"Still doesn't wash. She's here because her dad had a stroke, right? Basalind didn't con her into coming down here, or threaten her."

"All right. I'll bite." Chief Harris folded his arms. Jay only smiled at her. "Why now?"

Dani faced him. "She learned something new. Maybe something her dad told her?"

Harris gave his head a quick shake. "But he can't speak. Can't do much of anything from what I'm told."

"Right." Jay straightened. "My mom mentioned that Lauren had dealt with all sorts of obstacles to get access to his bank account so she could pay his mortgage and bills."

That was it. "She saw something in his bank account. That's the *why now* answer."

Harris picked up the phone receiver from his desk. "Appleby. Get ahold of Milford White... I know what time it is. I need a court order to open the bank account records of Frederick Stiles. Need it by nine A.M." He hung up abruptly. "See, I knew telling you about this little tidbit would work in my favor."

"What are you going to do about the sheriff?" Jay scowled. "And Kyle, who's still stuck in the man's lock-up?"

Harris gave his head a little shake. "Hard enough dealing with that man, but it may take an extra day, tomorrow being the Fourth and all."

Dani glanced back at the clicking clock. "Make that today."

Jay helped Dani into his truck in the now lit-up lot behind the StopNShop. The crime scene tape had returned, and flood lights illuminated the entire area. Two officers and a photographer still worked inside, but Jay had no desire to join them.

The hospital held the answers he needed. Kristi's status and Lauren's diagnosis. He had a feeling the latter was a little worse than the chief had led him to believe. Especially considering the amount of blood that had covered the cheap flooring.

"You're looking a little pale. You feeling all right?" Dani laid her soft hand on his arm.

He cranked up the engine. "Hard to swallow all of this."

"I know she was your… well, more than a friend."

He cut a hard turn and paused at the lot's exit. So many secrets. "She killed someone. Covered it up by hiding the body. How could I have missed that?"

"You haven't been around her." Dani's voice was soft. "Regardless, you can't blame yourself for not realizing that someone you cared about wasn't who you thought."

He took her hand and kissed her knuckles. "You're right. Glad I'm around you, now." He squeezed her hand and smiled at her, but her gaze drifted to the passenger window.

They rode in silence and made good time getting to the hospital. Mom and Dad again sat in the waiting room as Jay entered with Dani. Dad stood as they neared.

"Do we have any news?" Jay ushered Dani toward the couches.

"Anytime, now." Dad nodded at Dani. "You've been gone awhile. Did you get to see Kyle?"

If only. "Fowler wasn't having any of it."

"I didn't believe that he would." Dad reclaimed his seat. "He's been looking for us, though. I received a call from the pastor. Sheriff insinuated that he'd be harboring a fugitive if he didn't reveal where we were."

"Remind me to thank my sister for her timing." They both might be in jail otherwise. "I spoke to an attorney friend of mine. Kyle should be home today. Tomorrow at the latest." He winked at Dani. Thank heaven all of this was over.

"Who posted bond?" Mom leaned forward and

clutched at Jay's hand. "How long do we have to repay them?"

He knelt. Her forehead had grown new creases. "No bond. The charges are going to be dropped." Hopefully he could speak to his Texas Ranger friend and get an investigation going on the sheriff and his office. The man had to be dirty.

"How, why?" Dad stood. "I know Kyle didn't kill the man, but what has changed?"

Jay rose and wrapped an arm around Dani's shoulders. "Our girl here found out who really killed Roger Basalind."

Mom's eyes widened. "Are you all right, dear?"

"I'm fine." Dani smiled.

Thank You, God.

Dad lowered to the seat. "Tell us, please. What happened?"

Jay and Dani sat on the couch across from them. She gave him a sidelong look. "I guess the first thing we noticed was that they had finished with the crime scene."

Jay let her do most of the talking. The look of surprise on Dad's face almost made the danger worthwhile. Almost. She downplayed the danger factor though. "Dani clobbered Lauren with a hotdog cooker. Believe that?"

Mom chuckled. "I knew there had to be some sort of benefit from one of those things."

The automatic doors opened in prelude to Sheriff Fowler's arrival. "Caroline Hunter, you have the right to remain silent."

Dad stepped in front of Mom. "Wait a minute, Arthur. Why are you arresting my wife?"

"I'll arrest you, too, if you don't step out of the way."

Jay stood and eased Dad back. "Don't worry. You'll probably win enough from the lawsuit to pay the mortgage on the ranch."

Fowler laughed. "This isn't the big city, boy. Judges here don't look favorably on criminals filing trivial lawsuits."

"Add slander to the list." He pointed to a nurse at the counter. "You heard the sheriff just call my father a criminal, right?"

Her eyes widened, but she nodded.

"Truth is a perfectly fine defense."

Jay had to choke on the word truth coming from Fowler's lips. The man wouldn't recognize it covered with nametags. "Don't let me interrupt you, Sheriff. You were arresting my mom for the murder of Roger Basalind, right?"

He pulled out his handcuffs, but his eyes narrowed.

"The same murder for which my brother has been arrested?"

Fowler glared at Jay. Looked like he'd made the sheriff's list of hated Hunters. "As soon as things are processed, Kyle will be released."

"But, of course, today is a national holiday."

"I'm sure he'll be out by tomorrow sometime." A smirk claimed his mouth.

"Good. I'll add delayed adjudication to the

suit."

"No reason for a hearing if he isn't going to be tried."

"Exactly." Jay smiled and pulled out his phone. "Please, don't let me stop you. Slap the cuffs on Mom." He turned to the nurse. Two orderlies had joined her. "You all getting this?"

The nurse nodded. "Sheriff Fowler is arresting your mom for the murder of a Roger-somebody."

"I never said all of that." Fowler puffed.

One of the orderlies aimed his phone at the sheriff.

"Put that thing away." The sheriff tucked his cuffs back into his pocket.

"Are you going to arrest him as well?" A rancid taste rose in Jay's mouth. This man's only purposes for his position were retaliation and profit.

And his attacks on Jay's family were stopping here and now.

"I have plenty of evidence connecting your mother with the murder at the StopNShop."

"Circumstantial at best." Jay squared and faced the man. "Even you aren't completely convinced. That's why you've put away your cuffs."

"You sound like you want me to arrest her."

"I'd love it." Jay let his anger growl through his voice. "I'd have you out of office so fast, you'd lose your hat." Didn't look like the man would, at this point, though Jay still held out hope.

He hesitated, glancing from Jay to his parents. Then he stuck a beefy finger in his mom's face. "Don't leave the county."

Jay bristled. "She'll go wherever she wants, Fowler."

"I have an open investigation—"

"No!" Jay thundered. "*You* don't have any investigation. Chief Harris has one for which he has made an arrest."

"What are you talking about?" Fowler straightened.

"My brother better be out of your jail within the hour. That's what I'm talking about." Jay sneered, but kept his distance.

"I'll see about this." The sheriff spun, flailing his hands in the air. "And you better be where I can find you, Caroline Hunter, or so help me…." He exited in mid-fluster.

"I'm calling my Ranger friend with or without your blessing, Dad."

Chapter Fifteen

Dani watched Sheriff Fowler in the lighted entry in front of the Emergency Room. He spoke to someone on his phone. His neck reddened. Then he slammed the phone on the concrete.

What a waste.

Thankfully, he'd gone into the parking lot instead of returning inside. He'd have probably blamed the Hunter family for the loss of his phone as well.

"Are you all right?" Jay took his mom's arm and lowered her onto a cushion.

"Why would he want to arrest me?"

"You were at the StopNShop before the fire." Mr. Hunter had said as much.

Mrs. Hunter let her gaze falter. "I went to speak with Roger. The back door was open. I found him on the floor. So I left." She shut her eyes. "Finding someone like that... all I could do was escape."

"Because you thought your husband had killed him?" *Ugh.* Couldn't she just once think before asking uncomfortable questions or making thoughtless comments?

"Caroline, you didn't really think I killed the man." Mr. Hunter turned in his seat to face his wife.

"You were so angry. And you disappeared for such a long time on Friday." Her voice softened.

"I'd had a fight with the man at the ranch. Because Dani overheard it, I needed to let my anger go before coming home. Took a drive around Lake Bradley." He combed his fingers through his thick, graying hair, just like his son did.

"Kyle must have seen you." Jay sat across from his mom. "He admitted to starting the fire. He tried to eliminate the stab wounds by burning the body, but apparently he failed."

Mrs. Hunter shook her head. "He was trying to protect me. I was trying to protect your father."

"All because of secrets." Jay eyed his mom.

"You're right, son… and pride." Mom's eyes teared up. "This is foolishness. No more." Her voice broke.

"Caroline." Dad put a hand on her knee.

"No. No more." She stood and paced to one side before returning. "The secrets need to come out, now."

"Sweetheart." Dad went to her, but she shook her head.

"I should never have let you lie to protect me." Tears spilled to her cheeks.

More lies? *Uh-oh.* Dani didn't like the way that sounded. If only she could fade into the painted wall.

Lies? Protection? Jay's thoughts tangled. "Mom?"

She halted and looked at him, her face drooping and her dark hair grayer and frizzier than he remembered. "I was the one who got carried away, son. The gambling. I was the one who went to Shreveport with Callie Southern. Of course, she had no idea how much money I had lost."

Jay reeled, glad he'd taken his seat before Mom unloaded this revelation.

"Something like that..." Dani drew Jay's attention, while Mom and Dad turned toward her as well. "...even in the extreme, can happen to anyone."

Mom sat. "Thank you, dear, but I know better." Her face dissolved in a fresh layer of tears silently glistening down her cheeks.

Dani moved closer and sat beside Jay. "Mrs. Hunter, I've seen things like this before. Gambling, drinking, worse. Good people, godly people, can get pulled into desperate situations."

Mom shook her head and stared at the wall beside her.

Dani leaned forward. "The important thing for God's people is that they don't remain. They don't get comfortable with their sin. Plainly that's your case."

Mom's gaze rose to Dani's face and stayed there.

Leave it to his girl to put things in the right perspective. "We're not perfect, Mom. Certainly not before we're saved, but not even afterward. We're going to mess up. That's what grace is about." He felt strange saying as much. After all, she was the one who had taught him the Truth.

She nodded. "I know. And I know I have to find a way to forgive myself. Regardless, our family is about to be dragged through the mud. All of us, even you, Jay, will feel the sting of my stupidity."

"Then we'll stand together." Dad pulled Mom to her feet and drew her close, his arm around her waist. "Like we always have." His gaze fell on Dani. A tender look crossed his expression. "You will stand with us?"

Jay held out his hand.

Dani grinned at Dad, then took Jay's hand and stood beside him. "I'd be honored."

Dani startled awake. The hospital waiting room lights in this corner had been turned off, and thankfully Labor and Delivery had little business during the wee hours. At least the visitors had been few while she'd been conscious. She leaned up from the couch where she'd been using a blanket from Jay's truck as a pillow. Pulling herself to standing, she began to fold the thick, plaid cloth. Where was Jay?

"Hey, beautiful." He came around a corner carrying two steaming cups.

"Yeah, right." She combed her fingers through her hair several times, then accepted his offered cup. "Thanks so much."

"Mom and Dad are upstairs, but we didn't want to wake you." He took the blanket from her and folded it over his arm.

Was it over? "Is Kristi all right? The baby?"

"Apparently still in recovery, but she wants us all to meet her in her room." He led her to the elevator.

Dani slowed. "This is a family thing, Jay. Why don't I go get breakfast for all of us? I bet Mike is starving." She glanced toward the front windows. Still pitch black outside. "You do have a twenty-four-hour drive-thru somewhere around here, right?"

"Later." He caught her fingers and drew her inside the doors as they closed. "Kristi specifically asked for you to be there. And besides, as far as I'm concerned, you are family."

His words both warmed and worried her. "Jay, there's so much you don't know about me." So much she still couldn't tell him even if she wanted to. Which she didn't. Though delaying her truth seemed less and less fair to Jay.

And more and more difficult for her to maintain. But then none of that would matter when she finally heard back from Matthew.

Jay tapped the bottom of her chin with his forefinger. "Doesn't change how I feel about you. Besides." He smirked. "There's a lot you don't know about me, too. I can be nothing but trouble."

She chuckled, as much from nerves as from his ludicrous statement. "I'd love to see that."

He lifted an eyebrow. "You just might."

The doors opened on the third floor. Her stomach exploded into butterflies, much like it had just before she met the Hunters. "Are you sure your parents wouldn't rather meet their grandchild alone?"

"Mom texted me to get you some coffee and wake you up so you wouldn't miss this."

Still, she doubted, but at this point, she'd take what they offered. "If you're certain." She followed him down the hall, trying to stifle the squirm that the antiseptic smell gave her. Her only experiences with hospitals had been bad and worse. Hopefully, this trip would change that trend.

Jay pushed open the door. "Any news?"

"Any minute." His mom practically glowed. She reached for Dani's hand. "I'm so glad you could share in this celebration."

"Papa. I'm going to teach him to call me Papa." Mr. Hunter paced but wore a bright smile. "And he'll be a Yankee Doodle Dandy."

Born on July Fourth. Dani smiled and set down her coffee before sliding her bag from her shoulder. "I can't wait to see him."

Jay's cell phone rang out with a strange ringtone. His eyes widened. "Kyle."

His mother and father tensed as he put the phone to his ear.

"Are you all right?" Jay listened for a moment before a smile began to spread on his face. He put his hand over the phone. "Sheriff woke him up a few minutes ago and dumped him out the back door with his possessions."

"That man." Mrs. Hunter looked downright fierce.

"No worries, Mom." He paused and listened again. "Told you Dyson was a good guy. We'll see you when you get here." He slipped his phone into his pocket. "One of the deputies had already called his attorney, my friend who lives there in High Grove. Barry picked him up right away, just in case the sheriff wanted to make more trouble."

"And he would if he could." His dad tucked his hands into his pockets.

Hopefully the people of Colter County would be wiser during the next election.

Jay guided Dani to stand near the windows. Kristi's third-floor room overlooked a half-empty parking lot.

He kept his hand at her back and stood a little closer than normal in the small room. "Kyle should be here in a half hour."

"Thank you, God." Mrs. Hunter lifted her eyes and her hands toward the ceiling. "So what's going to happen to Fowler?"

"Nothing can be proved, Caroline." Mr. Hunter pressed his lips together for a moment. "Nothing will happen to him."

"Unless you run again next May." Jay gave his dad a sidelong look. "You can't live in fear of what the man will do."

"I guess he's already attacked my family."

"And he failed." Dani couldn't resist hammering that little tidbit of truth home. "Jay's right, Mr. Hunter. The Lord put you in a place perfect for your unique abilities. And He gave you a passion for justice. Turning your back on reclaiming that position would be tragic. Especially since the man who now holds the power has little integrity."

The man listened to her. Really listened. "Perhaps you are right."

"Here's your new addition." A nurse pushed

the door open wide while an orderly shoved a rolling bed into the room. Kristi, beaming, sat propped against the incline of the bed as Mike followed the nurse.

"Oh." Mrs. Hunter led the chorus of cooing, but Jay and Mr. Hunter definitely doted on the sleeping addition to the family.

Dani hugged the corner near the windows but enjoyed the sight. Such a devoted family, all adoring the cute, little, pink bundle. She wondered who would notice the unexpected blanket color first.

Several more minutes of oohs and ahhs continued before Jay's dad straightened. "Why is my grandson wearing pink?"

Mr. Hunter won the prize.

"Granddaughter, Dad." The little bundle gave a wide yawn as Kristi tickled her child's tiny fingers. "This was why I wasn't about to share my name idea with any of you."

"But the doctor said he thought it was a boy."

Mrs. Hunter didn't take her eyes off the child.

Kristi shrugged. "He was wrong. Please welcome Devan Joy."

A huge grin broke across Jay's face. "Really?"

What was with his goofy look? "Will you call her Devan or Joy?"

"Definitely Joy. To commemorate the atmosphere our family has always had. And I believe we will have it again."

Her parents both nodded.

"Where did Devan come from?" Dani peered at Joy's deep blue eyes that had barely opened.

"Are you kidding me?" Kristi glared at Jay. "You never even told her your name is Devon Jeremiah?"

"Too long of a name." Mrs. Hunter toyed with Joy's hand. "My father's name. We thought to honor him, but I simply couldn't call Jay by either of the names. So I used the initials."

"DJ, at first, then simply Jay." He stepped back and urged Dani in front of him. "Didn't mean to keep it from you, sweetheart. I don't think about it."

"I see." Of course he wouldn't think about his nickname from childhood as using an alias. He didn't have anything to hide.

"You would've found out eventually." Kristi winked in her direction.

Dani laughed, but heat crept up the back of her neck. She glanced at the faces in the room, lit with excitement and clearly enjoying each other's company.

What must it have been like to grow up in such an environment? What would it be like to be part of this family?

Jay turned his dazzling smile on her and reached for her hand. Pulling her close, he whispered in her ear. "I told you they would love you. Not as much as I do, though." He planted a kiss on her temple.

Worrying about losing Jay when he learned about all of her secrets only served to spoil the relationship they enjoyed in the present. For now, she'd delight in all the Lord had given her.

Chapter 1: GRIME & PUNISHMENT

Dani Foster munched on the last caramel Bugle chip like any twenty-something out with her favorite guy and tried to forget she was a Judas with a target on her back. Pulling her knees under her chin, she leaned against Jay's strong shoulder where he'd propped himself against the trunk of a tree. The cars on the busy road beneath them kept up a constant white noise.

Jay Hunter leaned close. "Want to walk off our dinner?" His warm breath tickled her ear.

Whatever you say. She shouldn't be so infatuated with this man. No, her feelings had gone way past infatuation months ago. In a perfect world, the two of them might actually have a chance of forever. But her world was far from perfect.

He pulled her to her feet and held her close. She let his half-smile capture her attention and let the moment linger until the raucous screeching of some bird interrupted her reverie. The most annoying sound worked perfectly as a ring tone for the most annoying person she knew. She shut her eyes and reached for her phone. No use in trying to ignore it, and doing so could put her and Jay both at risk.

She gave Jay and apologetic grimace. He didn't know everything, but he'd had to deal with her calls from Matthew Donaldson before. She swiped the screen. "You've got lousy timing, Matt." She took a few steps away from Jay, leaning against a tree to keep her balance on the steep incline.

"And you've got a lousy memory." Her witness protection agent had a sharp edge to his voice. "What happened to my instructions that you should contact me before leaving your apartment?"

Of course. Only one time in over a week that she had left without his permission, and he threw a fit. She lowered her voice to a whispered as she backed away a few more feet. "It's not like you aren't tracking me through my phone."

"Exactly. Stay there. I'm coming for you."

She caught Jay's eye and mouthed *I'm sorry* before turning her back. "Not exactly convenient timing right now."

"Not for me either, thank you very much. I'll meet you at the parking lot of Flag Pole Hill in twenty minutes." He clicked off.

"Wait! What?" She was speaking to no one at this point. He was coming here? What was the man thinking? That would mean she'd have to explain everything to Jay.

"Ready to walk?" He tucked the rolled blanket into his trunk and shut the lid.

"Absolutely." She'd have a good fifteen minutes to explain things gently. Well, as much as she was willing to share. She wasn't ready for him to completely hate her.

"I've been wanting to bring you back here for a while. Remember our first date?" He reached for her hand and helped her down the slope toward an easier path that would lead them back toward the way they had come.

"This is a perfect evening." Or it would be if the impending visit from Matt and the looming explanation didn't blot out her attempts to relish every moment with this man she adored.

"Hard to believe so much has happened since then."

So much. She'd almost lost him. The memory burned through her.

"I hope, now that you've quit your job at Kellerman's, you'll stay out of so many dangerous situations." He paused at the grassy shoreline.

Kellerman Crisis and Trauma Cleaners hadn't had anything to do with the events of the past several months. In truth, crime scene cleaning was tedious and would've been downright boring if she hadn't had her imagination weaving together stories about what she found on the job.

And as for putting herself into anymore danger, Matt had threatened to have her locked up. "I'm behaving." She stifled a chuckle as her five-year-old self said *I'm being-have* in her mind. Her nerves were letting in goofy thoughts. She fisted her one empty hand and braced herself to give a full explanation of her secrets.

"Good." He pulled her close. "I don't want to lose you. I've already been close to that, and I never want to go through it again." He stooped slightly and kissed her forehead. "You're precious to me, Dani. I can't imagine life without you." He took a step back. "And I want you to always be part of my life."

Still grasping one of her hands, he slowly lowered to one knee.

No. No. No. He couldn't be doing this. Not now with what she was about to tell him.

"Dani Foster." His gaze clung to hers and refused release.

Lord, this is going to break him. Why, why had she ever allowed herself to get serious with him in the first place. She was playing around with this man's heart, with his life.

"I want you to be my wife." He held up a solitaire

that caught the moonlight and sparkled.

Okay, she hadn't been playing, but she'd known this relationship would never last. Not once he knew the depth of her depravity.

"Will you marry me?"

She realized that her mouth had been hanging open slightly. She shut it without moving her gaze. Jay waited for an answer. An answer she wanted desperately to give. Didn't she have the right to happiness? After all, she'd given up her entire life, everything she loved from photography to going to church. Why did she have to give up still more?

"This is where you leap into my arms with a loud *yes* and plant a big kiss on my lips." His eyebrows raised and his grin grew.

The squeal of brakes and slamming car doors on the ridge above them startled her. "Are you sure she's here?" A man's voice. One she knew far too well.

"This is where the tracker led us. She has to be here."

Robert had found her.

Marji Laine

For Discussion & Study

1. Dani begins this story with so much stress. Meeting Jay's parents is bad enough, but Matthew's call reminds her of her unworthiness and the doomed relationship she's pursuing. What does Psalm 23 say about the way the Lord feels about us?

a. Do you ever feel unworthy? I know I do. I fuss at myself for every little mistake, using words like stupid and dumb. What does that do to you?

b. What does the Bible say about words? Proverbs 12:18, Proverbs 16:24.

Words are pretty big for me, so calling myself names is not my wisest move. But even with folks for whom words aren't as important, these Scriptures hold true.

2. It's important for us to view others through the Lord's eyes, dealing with them in the same love-actions that the Lord uses with us. Do you find it easier to show love to others than you do to yourself? I'm not heralding self-absorption or entitlement, but I do have trouble forgiving myself for mistakes. I tend to second guess things that I do and say. Surely, I'm not the only one! Here's what the Lord thinks about me: Psalm 139, Matthew 10:29-31, Psalm 8:4-5.

I can't help but think that Dani needs a refresher course in these verses.

3. Dani spent the entire book feeling guilt and a huge sense of foreboding about the eventual revelation of her secrets. I've come to the conclusion that her guilt is what is really keeping her from letting Jay know about her past. After all, others know, (from book 3) even Jay's partner, so the witness protection thing seems like an excuse to keep it from him. Is there any way that this pile of secrets she has doesn't blow up?

a. There are two types of secrets: those for someone else and those for yourself. Can you think of anything positive with either of those types of secrets?

b. I think secrets for someone else includes those that they've uttered as a type of confession: these can be dangerous. When we were young, we'd be more apt to tell our friends about our problems than our parents. But even as adults, we'll share things that can prove devastating for ourselves and our loved ones before we'll share bad news with our family. But at the same time, sometimes we're called on to keep secrets for others when they've needed the safety to vent and rid themselves of the uglies. So it can be a fine line we draw about whether to keep other's secrets. Can you think of another type of secret we might keep for someone else?

4. The secrets we keep for ourselves can also have positive and negative effects. I keep secrets that involve surprises. I keep nothing at all from my

sweet hubby and only temporary secrets from my kids. That way, they always know they can trust me. (Only talking about personal secrets here, not confidences.) Do you keep personal secrets from your friends and family? What type? What positive and/or negative effects do those secrets have on you? On them?

5. **SPOILER ALERT!** Did you have a clue about the antagonist? Some flaws in that person's character revealed themselves early on, but the secrets were devastating. Life changing. The antagonist had lived under the weight of a crime – a mere accident at the time – for over a decade, and the guilt and grief had taken a toll on other people as well. How might things have been different?

6. Keeping secrets can lead to sinister results as with the blackmail that Roger Baselind had going. It's crazy for me to think that situations like this actually exist. Especially when the word of one person, one victim whose secrets are more important than life itself, can halt all of the pain. Have you ever been held captive by your secrets? Maybe something in your past that necessitated the ending of a relationship or a job?

7. Read Luke 12:2 and Ephesians 5:6-13. What do these verses tell you about secrets? How does this story bear out that truth?

8. I think the passage mentioned at the beginning of this story, from Ephesians 5:15-16, not only sums up the theme of this book but defines how we are to be. How will these verses look in your life, with the things you're going through right now?

About the Author

Marji Laine is a homeschooling mom with twins still left in the nest. She spends her days driving teenagers to activities and special classes, snatching writing time as she waits in various parking lots. To be honest, writing is a vacation for her, ranking alongside game night with the family and birthday or holiday celebrations.

When she's not writing or game-playing, her nose is usually in a great book. She's the senior reviewer at Suspense Sisters. She also enjoys road trips, photography, scrapbooking, and participating in musical theater. She's the children's music director at her church, teaches a middle school girls Sunday School group, helps with the youth choir, sings in the adult choir, and is the webmaster and the high school coordinator for a large homeschool co-op.

You can find updates of her latest works in progress on the news section of her website at MarjiLaine.com. All of her books are listed on her Amazon Author page, and you'll learn more about her on her Facebook page.

If you enjoyed this story, please leave a review at the Amazon page, and be sure to collect the Grime Fighter series for all the elements of Dani and Jay's story. And be watching for the last book in this series, coming out in early 2017.

From the Author

Dear Reader,

I'm so glad you've joined me again for another of Dani's and Jay's mysteries. I'm going to be so sad to say goodbye to these characters, but the next book will be the final one of the series. Hopefully, they will weather the storm of secrets and deception.

I really think secrets are virtual IED's to any relationship. On the secret-keeper's side, they represent guilt or worry and force the keeper to stay on constant guard against revealing too much of their hidden domain. Like Jay's mom and dad. John and Caroline should have been honest with Jay at the beginning, knowing that out of sheer family devotion whatever affects them will affect him. Had they leveled with him before the visit, Jay wouldn't have likely included Dani in the trip at all, electing instead to come home and help his parents through their issues.

Would have totally messed up my story, but I think either way, their familial relationship would have been strengthened. As it was, however, the secret laid in a shallow pit under the surface. Jay's mom tried to dig it up several times, from multiple layers of guilt since her sweet husband insisted on bearing the blame. But instead, it lingered until the moment it was set off.

That blast hurt Jay most, since he didn't even realize there *was* a secret. And that's often the case for the one in the dark. When revelation comes, and it will for most people if the relationship has any hope of lasting, it happens like an ambush. The attack comes without warning or hint and blows up in the faces of both parties.

In fact, both get a double blast. The one in the dark has the POP that there is a secret and an immediate BOOM of what the secret is. The keeper endures the BOOM of revelation, but then has to stand against a softer CRACKLE, the pain that their secret has inflicted on their loved one.

As hard as honesty can be, it's imperative, especially if the relationship is treasured. And that brings me to the reaction we're supposed to have when secrets are revealed. Ephesians 4:31-32: "Get rid of all bitterness rage and anger, brawling and slander, along with every form of malice. Be kind and compassionate to one another, forgiving each other just as Christ forgave you."

Jay and Dani showed they had that kind of forgiveness in the story. Dani especially, since she knew the secrets she continues to carry have the strong potential to destroy every relationship she's made. But that's exactly the spot we're in. We know what Christ has saved us from. Sins that we'd be horrified to utter aloud. With that knowledge, how can we not forgive others who offend us?

This is not the "Oh, I've forgiven her/him, but I'll never forget." Or "I forgive you because God told me I must, but that doesn't mean I have to like you." True forgiveness is a sincere desire for God's best, His richest blessings, poured out on the offending person. Without reserve.

I've certainly been forgiven much! I've also been given excellent assistance through this story. I have a Dallas police officer to thank for answering my questions about procedure, particularly whether reactions would seem reasonable. I also want to thank several businesses in the town of Glen Rose, Texas, for their inspiration! Texas Treasures, Jitters Coffee Bar, Millie's Cottage, and Storiebook Café. Yes, they are real places and are downright delightful!

I'm also very thankful for my critique partners, Patricia Pacjac Carroll and Jackie Castle, who never let me get away with lazy writing. And who forgive me when I'm really tough on them! By the way, their names are linked to their Amazon Author pages. They are excellent Christian authors I can highly recommend whole-heartedly!

My proof-reader, Christa Upton, is point-on and gracious as always. I'm so in her debt! And I can't thank my family enough for urging me forward in my journey. And you, dear reader. I've heard from so many of you wanting to learn more about Jay and Dani and delighting in their exploits! Thank you for sharing your encouragement with me.

And I'm ever-so-thankful to my Father for sharing His words with me. May I spread a smile of delight across His face!

I'm praying for you, dear reader, that you may be inspired to know your Father more and more and grow to love Him deeper each day of your life!

Until next time,

Be Blessed!

Marji PS. Come visit with me at the places listed below or contact me at AuthorMarjiLaine@gmail.com!

Other Books from Marji Laine

Grime Fighter Mysteries
A Complete Series!

Working as a crime scene cleaner is perfect for neat-nick Dani Foster who has recently been relocated by her witness security contact. But she can't hide the investigative reactions drilled into her by her detective father. Even though her discoveries, and the explorations they instigate, often put her into funny, uncomfortable, and sometimes dangerous positions.

Heath's Point Suspense
COUNTER POINT – Book 1

Her dad's gone. Her business is in trouble, and her car's in the lake. Cat McPHerson doesn't have anything else to lose... except her life. And a madman is determined to take that.

Her former boyfriend, Ray Alexander, returns as a hero from his foreign mission, bringing back death-threats. Cat must find a way to trust Ray, the man who broke her heart or neither of them will survive.

BREAKING POINT – Book 2
Why would anyone want her dead?

Alynne Stone wanted nothing to do with her parents' inn after they left their lifelong home in Dallas to move to Heath's Point, Texas. Then an emergency phone call not only drew her to her parents' bed and breakfast, it thrust her into the crosshairs of a killer.

Lieutenant Jason Danvers has no idea why his kind and generous friend was killed. But the man's beautiful, prodigal daughter needs all the help he can give her to stay alive.

AIN'T MISBEHAVING

Book 1 of the
Dallas Duets Clean Billionaire Romance Series

Annalee Chambers: Poised, wealthy, socially elite. Convict.

She floated through life in a pampered, crystal bubble until she smashed it with a single word. Dealing with the repercussions of that word might break her, ruin her family, and land her in jail. That is, unless a handsome worker from the "other" side of the tracks, who has secrets of his own, can help her find her way.

www.ingramcontent.com/pod-product-compliance
Lightning Source LLC
Chambersburg PA
CBHW022019240626
47154CB00007B/2172